I0691499

WET DREAMZ

A Series of Erotic Bedtime Stories

EJ Barnes

"It's Time, for a book of sensual erotic bedtime stories. To arouse the sexual animal deep

Inside of you."

He whispered softy, reaching for her.

"Come, we have something to finish."

She moved closer to him, he looks her straight into her eyes.

"Are you ready? Are you ready for me?"

Placing his hand on her thigh and slowly inching closer.

"It's time to finish what we started"

His fingers inching their way to her inner thigh.

"Are you willing?"

He pulls her closer to him.

"To let me deep inside?"

He whispered into her ear as the passion intensified and he moved in to kiss her luscious sweet lips.

"Tell me, Are you? Tell me now"

His mouth now on her neck, their breathing coincide.

"Say it "

He grabs at her hair, a desire untied

"Are you mine? Show me now"

Her back arches as her legs part in reply.

She moans and looks deep into his eyes.

"I'm yours. I'm all yours Master"

Her eyes now shut tight, a sight sublime

"Now my love, I'm ready"

She said.

"it's time."

Trucking

She watched him, she craved him, wanting to please him. Headlights bounced off the windshield as he drove down the highway.

She knew he was getting tired, yet she ached to make him happy. She ached to relax him in a way only she could.

She sat, silent, watching him and starving for his body. The moonlight shining in distance over the mountains, as he pulled off into the truck stop and parked the truck. She knew he was exhausted, she gently rubbed his shoulders and kissed his lips. He quivered as her tongue ran across the back of his neck and up to his ear. He turned to her, kissed her then reached into her shirt unlatching her bra.

"Take off your top, NOW!"

He demanded with a growl.

She took off her shirt revealing herself to him, he grabbed her breasts, he squeezed them hard, then sucked on her nipples and bit her hard leaving marks. Having her half naked in front of him, turned him on in a way, that was almost animal like. She was starving for him, he was all that could cure the starvation now raging through her aching loins.

He reached for her and pulled her closer. Then tearing down her pants he demands,

"get on the bed NOW! My sexy little slut."

Her naked body now begging for him, as he takes his clothes off moves towards her, with an animal like glare in his eyes.

He leans in, kisses her then grabs her pussy hard and slides on to the bed.

His hands all over her body, as she shivers with his touch. He demands, " Get down there and suck my cock!" Then slaps her across the ass and bites it hard as she moves down.

She moves down and takes his already hard cock into her hand. She strokes it and runs her nails all the way down, right down to a spot that makes him quiver with pleasure and brings out the animal inside of him.

Then leaning in, She pushes his long hard cock into her mouth. She sucks him, hard and fast. Faster and faster while stroking his warm balls with her hand. He pushes her head, ramming his cock further into her mouth gagging her.

His body sweaty and quivering as she continues sucking him pushing him deep into her mouth. He can barely stand it anymore, his body ready to explode. Forcing himself further into her mouth. She then slowly pulls up and licks just the tip teasing him further as she then slides down and begins to suck on his balls. He's now shaking and moaning, he can barely stand it anymore.

He pulls away, grabbing her hard.

"Roll over now!"

He growls as He rolls her over and drives his throbbing cock deep into her hot soaked pussy. He drives it hard and fast, deeper and deeper with each thrust.

"Take it, take all of it"

he says. Now So deep inside of her, it's as if their bodies are one.

The passion's exploding as she can no longer contain the sounds of pleasure that shoot from her throat. He continues to go harder and harder, their bodies pressed hard together. She grips on to the pillow and screams as her body is taken over, all in his control.

He smacks her thigh as he says
"it's my turn, roll over!"

She rolls over and he quickly moves
to her ass.

He pushes his hard cock inside of her. It's dry and it hurts. She grips on to the pillow, so tight that you can see the whites of her knuckles. Seeing this brings out his inner animal and he drives himself a little deeper then stops, catching their breath for a brief second before he rams himself harder and harder until he's all inside of her. She's moaning and screaming, a mix of pain and pleasure, her body now his. His body shaking as the pleasure intensifies. He pushes deeper and harder and faster and faster. The harder he goes the louder the cries shoot from her throat.

She cries out

"I'm yours master, I'm all yours"

As sounds of pleasure now echo through the truck.

He moves faster and harder, his body filling with pure erotic animal pleasure. He moans as he gets closer and closer. He pushes even deeper.

"Take me, take it all"

he demands, slapping her ass. She screams and grips the pillows harder, her body completely over come. He reaches forward and puts his hand over her mouth. She takes his finger into her mouth and begins to suck it, as the cries continue to shoot from her throat.

Their bodies now shaking, she screams, he groans. Pushing faster and faster until he finally explodes deep inside of her., completely filling her ass with his cum. Their bodies as one, sweaty from the pleasure as he pulls out and she rolls over. He leans in to kiss her.

"I love you"

She whispers softly

"I love you to"

Seductive Starvation

She craved him, all of him. His mouth, his seductive voice, his chest and beating heart.

She was alone, Silent and starving for his body. She lay naked in the moonlight aching for his touch.

Food no longer nourished her body. Nothing but him could cure the starvation that raged through her body and throbbing pussy.

Then suddenly, the rising sun disrupts her, another night has passed. Her mind drifts to him, with visions of his naked body walking towards her.

She reaches for him and pulls him closer. Her naked body begging for him. He leans in grabs her by the throat, kisses her and slides into her bed.

His hands all over her body, as she shivers with his touch.
"Do you want me?" He asks
"Tell me, beg for me"

She looks into his eyes
"Yes Master, I want you. Please Master"

He looks down at his already hard cock then nods to her and Replies

" you know what to do then"

She reaches down and takes his hard cock into her hand. She strokes it and runs her nails up and down, she takes his balls into her hand strokes them while slowly licking his cock up and down making him quiver as his animal like nature begins to emerge.

She's teasing him, she moves closer and runs her nails up and down his entire body. Then moving back to his cock, she pushes him deep into her mouth. She sucks him, hard and fast. Faster and faster while stroking his warm balls with her hand. The animal in him now taking over, as he rams his cock further into her mouth. She gags, as his pushes himself deep into her throat over and over.

His body sweaty and quivering as she's taking him deeper and deeper. He can barely stand it anymore, his body ready to explode.

He slaps her ass and pulls her hair while continuing to ram his cock deep into her throat. She's stroking his balls and teasing him with her nails as his body begins to convulse and his hot cum shoots down her throat.

"Swallow it my sexy slut, swallow it all "

He says as he pushes her head one last time, and begins driving himself in and out of her throat, once again getting himself ready for more.

Then slapping her ass, he demands
"get on your knees"

She get's on her knees, her soaked pussy now aching for him.

He gets up behind her and drives his throbbing cock deep into her hot soaked pussy. He pushes it hard and fast, deeper and deeper with each thrust. He's so deep inside of her, she can barely breath as she screams with a mix of both pleasure and pain, he's all inside of her, she squirms her breathing out of control as the pleasure takes over and she cums all over his cock. Feeling her cum, makes him even harder. His animal

urges now unleashed

She can no longer contain the sounds of pleasure that shoot from her throat He pushes harder and harder, so deep she can barely take it, their bodies as one.

He pulls out and smacks her ass, then leans down and bites it hard. Leaving his teeth marks behind.

Then quickly moves to her ass. Her ass is dry, but it doesn't stop him. He starts to push his hard cock inside of her. It hurts, she screams and tries to pull back. He grabs her hips and pulls her to him.

"Don't pull away"

he demands.

"Who owns you?"

He asks.

Gripping the pillow hard as he continues to push himself further into her ass.

"You do sir. I'm all yours Master"

Her body is shaking with the pain as he pushes himself further. His body taken over with pure animal pleasure as he rams it deeper and deeper, harder and faster.

She moans and her cries echo through the room. Now not just with pain but pleasure too.

He moves faster and faster, his body filling with pure pleasure, he moans as he gets closer and closer. Seeing her clenching the pillows so tight, as he pounds her tight ass, brings him a satisfaction like no other. His animal nature takes over and he rams himself even deeper until he's so deep inside of her she can't take no more.

Their bodies shaking, she screams, he groans. Pushing faster and faster. She knows he's close, she feels his throbbing cock ready to burst deep inside her ass. He's groaning, his body now convulsing as the hot cum shoots from his cock and completely fills her ass.

He pulls out slowly, his cum dripping from her ass. She rolls over, sweaty and out of breath as he leans down and kisses her.

With that, she's startled by a noise in the room.

Her panties now soaking wet, from what had been nothing more then an erotic fantasy

Dirty Little Housewife

Walking into the kitchen, he pauses when he sees her. There she is, in her tight little denim shorts, down on her knees washing the floor. Her hair pulled back in a messy bun, sweaty from the heat. Her heart shaped ass in the air, moving from side to side enticing him.

He only came in to grab a beer, but the sight of her, stopped him dead in his tracks. He can't help but watch her, in his pants his cock is now hard. He wants her, he wants to feel her lips wrapped around his cock. He wants to feel the back of her throat as he chokes her with it. He walks up behind her and smacks her ass then squeezes it hard. She looks up at him, knowing what it is he wants.

She turns to him still on her knees, unzips his pants and takes his cock into her hand and begins to stroke it.

He grabs her hair and tips her head back, leans down and kisses her.

"Suck my cock you dirty little whore"

he demands.

She leans in

"Yes Sir"

Then takes his cock into her mouth and begins stroking it in and out while squeezing and rubbing his balls with her hand. She's sucking him fast, then slow, then fast again. Then sliding up to the tip, popping off and teasing the tip with her tongue.

His body being taken over with pleasure, as he pushes the back of her head. Ramming his cock deep into her throat gagging her. He gags her so hard tears fill her eyes. He keeps going, pushing his cock hard in and out of her mouth gagging her each time. He's getting close as he pulls out

"Suck my balls"

He demands, pushing her head down.

She begins to suck on his balls and runs her tongue down to that one spot, she knows gets him wild.

His body begins to quiver, he's getting closer. He's moaning, his legs now shaking.

"Suck my cock, suck it NOW!"

He groans as he grabs her hair pulling her up and ramming his cock back down her throat. She sucks it hard and fast. Deeper with each stroke, his body completely overcome. Then just as he's ready to blow his load deep into her throat. He pulls out and shoots his hot cum right on her chest and it runs down her tank top into her hot sweaty cleavage. She reaches in and wipes it off with her hand then licks her hand clean, while he watches.

"That's my girl"

He says , as he zips his pants back up.

" when you're finished the floor, meet me on the sofa. I'm not finished with you yet."

She smiles and raises her eyes brows, with an enticing, flirty look. Then goes back to scrubbing the floor.

He grabs his beer and goes back into the other room.

Once finished in the kitchen, she heads in to meet him. She walks towards him slowly, seeing her coming he growls and says.

"Top still on? Lose it!"

She takes her top off and joins him on the sofa. He grabs her breasts and
squeezes them

So hard it hurts. He leans in and bites her, his teeth marks now there like a little
calling card.

Then pulling her closer, he reaches into her shorts.
" Mhmm you're so wet, your panties too. That's my dirty little whore"
He says as he unzips her shorts and yanks them down.
"Turn over, lean over the back of the sofa"
 he says while smacking her ass hard.

She leans over the sofa, her ass in the air. He slaps it hard again and moves
in and bites it.

Then pulling her closer he leans down and licks her already soaked pussy, while
fingering her hard and deep. She's getting wetter, her pussy throbbing with
pleasure, his warm tongue getting her closer and closer and ready to cum as he
continues stroking his fingers faster and faster in and out of her.
"Cum my little slut, cum"
He groans while licking and fingering her faster and faster.
"I want to taste you, cum for me, cum for me now!"
He demands.
Hearing his demands, gets her hotter and hotter, her pussy throbbing and ready to
explode. She can no longer contain herself as the sounds of pleasure shoot from
her throat. Her body begins to shake, waves of pleasure taking over as he
continues eating out her hot soaked pussy, his face now dripping wet from her. He
knows she's close, he fingers her faster and licks her clit. She's grabbing on to the
sofa her body shakes, she can barely breath as she bursts into massive orgasm
and screams with pleasure.

She sighs an unintentional sigh of relief as she tries to catch her breath.

He leans in to her, grabs her face and kisses her.

"I love you"

She looks into his eyes and smiles in reply.

The slutty Step-Mom

Walking past her room, he could hear the subtle vibrations of her vibrator. Her door not quite closed all the way, so he stops to peek in.

There she is, naked on her bed, spread eagle. Slowly stroking her vibrator in and out of her pussy, while rubbing and squeezing her breasts.

He can't help but watch as he feels his cock getting harder and harder in his pants. He's always crushed on her, jealous of his father knowing he has her. Ever since the day she and his father married. He's watched her, wanting her. Noticing her watching him too. It wasn't just a glance here and there, she watched him, like she wanted him too.

As he watched her playing with herself, he reached into his pants and began stroking his cock. Then getting lost in the moment, he leaned into the door causing it to creek. She stopped, noticing him there. Then to his surprise, she asked him in.

"Instead of watching, why don't you join me?"

He was nervous, he'd wanted this for so long, was it really happening?

He walked in and over to her bed, there she was before him, completely naked. His cock rock hard and at this point impossible to hide.

She smiles looking at the bulge in his pants.

"Is that for me?"

He looked into her eyes

"Yes Ma'am"

At this point he was ready to burst, he wanted her so badly.

"What about my Father? What if he comes home?"

She pulled him close to her reaching into his pants.

"He's at work, won't be home for hours. Do you want me?"

He moaned sliding off his pants.

" yes, yes I do."

She pulled him on to the bed with her, then as he lay there, naked with his

cock hard and ready for her. She straddled him, with her pussy just above his

face.

"Eat my pussy, eat it like a starved rabid animal"

She said pushing herself closer to his mouth as she leaned down and

began sucking his cock.

Pushing his cock deep into throat, sucking him and licking him, teasing him

with her tongue.

While he licked her wet pussy, sucked her clit and buried his tongue deep inside

of her to taste the hot juices of her desire.

He was shaking, nervous his father would walk in yet at the same time, the

thrill of being caught sent an erotic sensation coursing through his body.

She sucked him long and fast, he could feel the tip of his cock hitting the

back of her throat and hear her gag each time. Her pussy now so soaked, it drips on his face. He keeps licking her, ferociously as she squirms above him, ready to cum.

She's moaning and panting as she gets close, now sucking his cock even faster. Then as he sucks her clit, his face is suddenly soaked as her moaning intensifies and she cums all over his face.

Hearing the erotic sounds shooting from her and filling the room. Brings him to a level of intense passion that he could no longer contain. He begins to shake and writhe about below her as his hot cum begins to shoot deep down her throat.

Then he watches her as she swallows and licks every drop.
"Mmm that's a good boy."
She says as she slides off of him.
"Do you want more? Do you want to pound my wet pussy?"

Hearing the words coming from her mouth, turned him on, his cock once again beginning to get hard. She grabbed it and starting stroking it.
"Answer me, do you want my pussy wrapped around your cock?"

He moaned as he looked into her eyes.
" Yes Ma'am"

His cock now hard again, as she gets on top of him and pushes him deep inside of her and begins riding him. Slow, then fast then slow again. Her long hair dangling down the sides of his face. He reaches up and grabs her breasts, he squeezes them hard and pinches her nipples. She leans further forward pushing them into his face, he grabs on with his mouth.

He sucks on her nipples and bites them gently. She's moaning and sweating as she rides him faster and faster, driving him hard and deep inside of her.

She's about ready to cum, as she starts moving her hips in a circular motion, twisting him deep inside of her. Faster and faster, screams of pleasure shooting from her throat.

He's knows she's about to cum, he grabs her breasts harder then bites on to her nipple and teases it with his tongue.

She begins to shake, her body now out of her control as she slows and she cums on his rock hard cock still deep inside of her.

Then pulling off of him, she gets on her knees.
"Come on, it's your turn. Finish up!"
He comes up behind her, pulls her close and drives himself back inside of her. He's so deep inside of her, he can feel the back of her pussy. Then as he pounds her pussy hard and deep she moans
"Smack my ass, smack it hard!"

Hearing her demands, he smacks her ass then leans down and bites it.

While continuing to pound her pussy, harder and harder.

She's now almost screaming as she shouts out.

" I want you to pound my ass, do it, do it now!"

He's never done that before, but the thought of it aroused him even further, as he pulled out of her pussy and moved to her ass.

Then sliding his fingers into her pussy, he used her own cum to wet her ass then slowly pushed himself inside.

She screamed as his pushed harder and harder to get inside of her. He slowed down unsure if the screams were pain or pleasure.

She moaned

"No don't stop, just do it, pound my ass!"

With that he pushed his cock harder ramming it all the way into her ass. He was so deep inside of her, it was tight around his cock. It was different, a different feeling then he'd ever felt before. It turned him on in way that made him completely lose control of his senses as he began pounding her, harder and harder. She was screaming and panting, cries shooting from her throat, she grabbed on to the pillows and buried her face in them trying to muffle the sounds.

His body now completely overcome, he moans loudly with one final slam into her ass. Then begins to shake and his hot cum shoots deep inside of her.

Then pulling out, he lays on the bed next to her.

She rolls over and kisses his cheek.

"Better get cleaned up before your Father gets home."

He's completely blown away by what's just happened. As he gets up from the bed and puts his pants back on.

Then as he turns to walk away, she grabs him and whispers in his ear.

"He's working over time all week."

Sunday Dinners

Sunday dinner, the family all together and gathered around the dinning room table.

They hadn't been together in months, he hadn't seen her since she moved out on her own and he in with his girlfriend.

He had always been drawn to her in a way that was forbidden. She was his step sister, they had grown up together, through their teens, like true siblings. There was something about her though, something more. Then with any of the others. It was a raw sexual attraction that made him ache for her, every time he looked into her eyes.

He stared across the table at her. Watching her eat, wishing it was him she was putting into her mouth. She feels him staring, as she looks across to him, grins snd winks. Then under the table, reaches for his foot with hers and then runs her toes up his leg. This was a first, she was making her move and flirting right back. Unsure what to think, he reaches back with his foot, running it up her leg, as she had done to him. She raises her eyebrows, looking towards him in a flirty seductive fashion. Then nods to him and looks towards the door, as she gets up. Signalling him to follow her.

He waits for her to leave the room, then gets up from the table and goes after her, unsure exactly where she went, he looks around the corner into the other room, but she's not there. He continues to look, when suddenly she comes up behind him giggling and grabs a hold of him.

"Did I scare you?"

She says as she kisses the back of his neck and starts to suck on his earlobe.

"No, I wasn't sure where you went."
He said, as the feeling of her sucking his ear sent shivers down his spine.

Then moving to his lips, she kissed him. This was definitely not a sibling kiss. It was a passionate kiss, long and hard burying their tongues in each other's mouths.
He moaned as he reached and cupped her breasts in his hands, squeezing them hard.

"What are we doing? Can we do this?"
He asks.

As she grabs him by hands, leading him away.
"Come with me."

Then she leads him outside to the pool house in their yard.
"In here, nobody will see or hear anything."

With that she takes off her top, revealing herself to him.
"I've wanted you for so long, but wasn't sure you'd return the feelings"

He takes his shirt off and grabs her. Pulling her body up against his.

Her nipples now hard, as they're pressed against him. His cock getting harder and harder in his pants.

She gets down on her knees and unzips his pants and reaches in to pull out his hard cock.

"Mmm you're ready for me"

She says as she starts to stroke it and leaning in gently kisses the tip, teasing him and making him want to be inside of her.

She looks up at him, with lust in her eyes.

"What do you want? Tell me?"

She says

As she runs her tongue up and down his hard cock.

He grabs her by the hair, pulls her head back and kisses her. Then pushing her back down and shoving his cock back in her face.

He replies

"First, I want to ram my cock into your mouth, then we'll go from there."

She moans as she pushes his cock into her mouth and then let's him take over.

He rams it in and out of her mouth deep into her throat. Her eyes tearing as she gags over and over. The sounds of her gagging makes him hotter. He grabs on to the sides of her head. Holding her there while he moves faster in and out of her mouth. His body tingling with the sensation of her tongue and the heat of her hot breath. He's ready to cum, as his body starts to shake.

"I'm about to cum, I'm going to cum right down your throat."

He says with a groan.

She moans and strokes his balls with her hand. While waiting to taste him.

He starts to slow down, his body begins to shake as his thrusts begin to jerk and hot cum, spurts from his cock and right down her throat and she swallows it all. Watching her swallow his hot cum, arouses him further. His cock starting to once again get hard.

She takes him in her hand and begins stroking him up and down.

" I want you to pound me, punish my dirty little pussy, with your hard cock!"

She says, as she turns around with her ass towards him. So he can take her from behind.

He moves in close, squeezes her ass hard and smacks it. Then slightly spreads her legs and pushes his fingers into her now soaked pussy.

"You're so wet"

He says, pulling his fingers out and licking them.

She moans and pushes herself closer to him.

"Punish my pussy, punish it now!"

She cries out wanting him deep inside of her.

His cock now rock hard, throbbing and aching to be inside of her.

Her grabs her by the hips, pulls her to him and rams his cock deep inside of her. Pushing it long and hard, until he can't go any further. His cock completely fills her pussy as he starts ramming it in and out of her. Fast, then slow. Then pulling nearly all the way out, teasing her with the tip and ramming it all the way back in. She screams as her passion takes over. Her body tingling with the feeling of his cock filling her soaked pussy.

"Pound me, pound me hard! Punish my pussy, punish it"

She cries out, making him push harder and deeper inside of her.

He's now going so hard and so fast, it's hard to tell where one stroke ends and the other begins.

She's screaming as her pussy begins to throb and the waves of pleasure take over her body.

He knows she's about to cum. Her pussy now dripping wet and soaking his cock.

He moves faster, then slow as now both their bodies are ready to explode.

Then as she's about to cum, she cries out

"Yes, yes pound me pound me hard. I'm cumming, I'm cumming on your cock."

Then with the feeling her pulsing orgasm deep inside her pussy, he begins to shake and he himself cums deep inside of her.

They're both moaning and out of breath as he pulls out . Her pussy dripping, filled with their cum.

"We better get cleaned up before we get caught"

He says reaching for his pants.

She gets up and starts to put her clothes back on.

"Sunday dinners at home, just got a lot more interesting!"

She says.

Then as she turns to head out of the pool house. She stops and whispers in his ear.

"Same place next Sunday?"

He growls and smacks her ass.

"You bet!"

Co-Ed showers

Steam fills the room, sounds of water pouring down like rain on a roof top. There she stands, completely naked, her body covered in soap suds. She's in the shower, the hot steamy water. Pouring down on her body, as she's washing herself, unaware that he is watching her.

It's a Co-Ed shower room, but the men rarely come in while the women are there. She continues washing her body, soaping up her breasts and reaching down to wash her dirty little pussy. All the while, he's there. Watching her while stroking himself.

Another girl notices him and walks over to her and taps her on the shoulder.

"You're being watched"

As she points in his direction.

Seeing her looking, he moves to the side, thinking he's out of sight as he continues to watch her.

She smiles seductively,

"Hmm he likes to watch does he? Let's give him a show then."

She says turning around, so she's facing his direction.

She starts squeezing her breasts and playing with her nipples. Licking and biting her lips. The hot steamy water pouring off of her, her body dripping wet. She's getting hot, knowing that he's watching her. As she leans up against the shower wall and she reaches between her legs and starts playing with her pussy. Pushing her fingers inside of herself and encircling her clit with her finger tips.

His cock rock hard, as he watches her. Wanting so badly to join her. Her pussy becoming soaked as the thoughts of him watching her, turned her on in way so hot that she was ready to burst. She fingered herself faster and faster, now ready to cum as she bites her lips and moans. Her body tingling and convulsing as the waves of pleasure take over and she cums on her own fingers.

Then looking in his direction, knowing he's stroking himself, she signals to him with her finger and says.

"Do you want some help with that?"

Looking over to her with a seductive glare in his eyes, he moans and replies.

"Mmhmm yes please."

Then he walks over to join her.

She's pushes her body up against his, an athlete, he's built and tanned with a six pack. His body glistening as the water rolls off of him. She runs her nails down his chest, he grabs her ass hard and moving to her breasts. He leans down and begins to suck and bite at her nipples, now rock hard from his touch.

She moans and licks his body, running her tongue all the way down to his cock. Then pushing him into her mouth, she begins sucking him, pushing him deep into her throat.

Off to the side, the other girl watches. Seeing them go at each other, makes her hot, as she begins playing with herself while watching them.

His body being taken over with the sensation of her throat hitting the tip of his cock.

He grabs on to her head and begins pushing himself, now taking over. He's ramming his cock in and out of her mouth. He's so deep she gags. Her eyes water and mascara runs down her face. He's moaning, his body twitching with pleasure, he's about to cum. She grabs his balls in her hand and begins rubbing them increasing the intensity of his arising orgasm. He begins to jerk, his body tingling. As he pulls out and shoots his hot cum all over her face.

Then wanting more, he pulls her up and gets down on his knees. Pulls her close and begins licking her soaked pussy, pushing his tongue deep inside of her and nibbling ferociously at her clit. His cock becoming hard again, as he tastes her cum deep inside of her. She's about to cum again, as her legs start to shake and she leans into the wall.

He starts fingering her, moaning.

"That's it, cum for me! Cum for me you dirty little girl."

Hearing his demands, turns her on as the waves of pleasure take over. Knowing she's about to cum, he rams his tongue deep inside of her. She starts panting and moaning, her body shaking as she bursts into massive orgasm all over his face and he licks it all up.

" Mhmm good girl"

He says as he smacks her ass. His cock now rock hard again and wanting more.

"Up against the wall, turn around"

He demands

She turns to the wall, the water still pouring down on their hot bodies.

He grabs her ass and pulls it to him.

Then separating her legs just enough, he spreads the cheeks of her ass and reaching into her pussy, he uses her own cum to get it nice and wet.

"Brace yourself"

He says, as he starts to push himself into her ass.

"This is going to hurt."

He starts to push harder, it hurts as she starts to groan through the pain. He keeps going, pushing harder and harder. Tears streaming down her face. He's now all inside of her, his cocks fills her ass so tight as he starts ramming her long and hard. She's panting and groaning. It hurts but at the same time pleasure takes over her body. He's going faster and faster. She reaches down and starts to play with her own clit. While he continues pounding her ass. Her body tingling, the feeling I of him deep inside of her ass, mixed with the pleasure of her now awakened pussy

As she encircles her clit with her fingers, bringing herself to cum once again. She's squirming and panting as her pussy cums and causes pulsations through her ass that drive him wild. He's now moaning and groaning. His body completely taken over. He smacks her ass hard.

"Oh yea take it, take it, take all of me!"

He moans as he loses total control of his body

And his thrusts slow.

Then with one final ram, deep into her ass, he cums deep inside of her. Then as he pulls out, he looks over to see the other girl, pressed hard against the shower wall. Fingering herself and playing with her breasts.

"I think we had an audience"

He says, as he leaned in and kissed her cheek.

She smiles as she looks over.

"It seems like she enjoyed it."

He grins.

" Yes I would say so!"

Then grabbing her ass and kissing her once again on the cheek. He whispers.

"Until next time."

And he walks away.

The Naughty Sitter

Walking over, he gently shakes her shoulder.

A single father, home from a night out with the boys, to find the sitter asleep on the sofa.

Not his usual sitter, she couldn't make it. So sent her older sister in her place.

A beautiful University student, long blonde hair that gently lay across her face as she lay there sound asleep, with moonlight shining in through the window. She looks so peaceful and beautiful, he almost doesn't want to wake her, as he gently gives her one more shake.

She lifts her head and rubs her eyes.

"I'm sorry, I guess I fell asleep."

She says starting to get up.

He puts his hand on her shoulder.

"No worries, any problems tonight?"

She looks up at him, a handsome older man with a killer smile.

"Nothing to report, all good."

Then she starts to get up from the sofa and stumbles.

He grabs her

"Still not quite awake?"

He says, looking into her eyes.

His sexy blue eyes gave her shivers, as she replied

"I suppose I'm not."

He looks at the clock, heading towards the kitchen.

" Well, it's not all that late. Do you want to join me for a coffee before you head out?"

She stuttered to answer, she was attracted to him in a way that almost scared her.

"Umm ahh yea sure, that sounds good."

She said as she followed him into the kitchen.

Then as she watched him, standing at the counter making their coffee. Her mind drifted to thoughts of him, thoughts of him without his shirt, then thoughts of him completely naked. Thoughts of them together. Her heart now pounding in her chest, she can feel her panties get wet as she imagines him touching her.

She's completely zoned out and doesn't notice him handing her a coffee.

"Are you okay?"

He says.

Startled she looks up, reaches for her coffee and her hand touches his.

"Umm yea I'm great."

She answers, even though her mind is lost thinking about what she wanted to do to him.

She wants him, she wants all of him, but she's unsure how to make her move.

He's older and she just the sitter, a student not yet even twenty.

She looks in his direction staring, watching him, him noticing her watching, he smiles a seductive grin. Then looking into her eyes, he says.

"You have beautiful eyes."

She blushes and nervously replies

"Thank you, so do you."

Shocked at her response, he spills coffee on his shirt and jumps up.

"How clumsy of me."

He says headed to sink to wash it off.

She jumps up.

"Here, let me help you."

Then trying to dab out the coffee stain, she starts unbuttoning his shirt.

"Here, might be easier if we take that shirt off.

He's looking down at her, watching her slowly unbuttoning his shirt. Her heart racing as shes revealing his chest and her hand touches his body.

Then lost in the moment, she slowly runs her hand down his chest and leans into him. He puts his hand under her chin and tips her face towards him, leans in and kisses her.

Then looking into his eyes, she whispers.

"I want you."

He kisses her again.

"I want you too."

He whispers back, while grabbing her ass and giving it a squeeze.

She steps back and takes off her top, then her bra. Standing there before him, her nipples hard and wanting to be touched. He reaches for her, he grabs them. Squeezes them hard and pinches and twists her nipples. She's quivering with his touch, shivers running down her spine. He leans down, then shoving her breast into his mouth, he begins sucking and biting it. She moans and she reaches into his pants and takes his hard cock into her hand and begins stroking it. Then him, sliding down her body, he moves to her jeans and slips them off. Then slides his hand into her moist panties.

"Mmhm you're wet for me."

He says as he slides his fingers inside of her.

She leans into the counter, trying to contain herself, as he strokes his fingers in and out of her now soaked pussy.

Her legs starting to shake, her heart pounding as he scoops her up and sits her on the edge of the counter. Then slides her panties all the way off.

She moans, her body aching for him.

"I want you Sir, I want you bad!"

She says as he leans down and starts eating out her tight little pussy.

Pushing his tongue deep inside of her, in and out. Tasting her, while she squirms before him. Then switching to his fingers, he starts driving them hard in and out of her while licking and sucking her clit. Her body overcome with pleasure, she pants and moans and she cries out.

"Yes, yes oh yes!"

Her body shaking, she can barely hold herself up as she's overcome by the sensations of her arising orgasm. He goes faster and faster burying his face in her pussy. Her body completely out of her control as she starts to cum. She screams and pants, her body shaking. His face now soaked and dripping from her as he pushes his tongue deep inside of her to taste her sweet sweet cum. Then completely lost in the moment, she cries out.

"I want you Sir, I want you now! Screw my pussy, screw it hard. My body is yours."

Then slipping down off the counter she turns around she bends over, pushing her pussy up against his rock hard cock.

"Take me, take me Sir!"

She cries.

He moans, slaps her ass hard then leans down and bites it. Leaving behind his teeth marks or her tight little ass.

Then pushing forward, he takes her. So lost in the moment, he doesn't take it slow. Instead he rams his hard cock deep into her soaked pussy. He rams it so hard she screams with pain. It doesn't stop him, he keeps going. Ramming it over and over. He's so deep the tip of his cock his hitting the back of her pussy. Screams of pain being forced from her throat with each thrust. She's laying across the counter, at this point unable to hold herself up. Gripping the edge so tight that her knuckles are white. Her face now streaked from tears causing her mascara to run. He's pounding her over and over, the sight of her gripping the counter so tightly turning him on and bringing out his inner animal. He smacks her ass hard.

"Take it, take it you naughty little girl! You like it don't you? Tell me, tell me you like it!"

He demands.

Barely able to catch her breath, she cries out.

"Yes Sir, yes I do! Pound me, pound me hard!"

Hearing her cries, he pushes harder and harder ramming her so hard she's unable to control her body. She's shaking, moans being forced from her throat and echoing through the room. His body shaking, as waves of pleasure course through him. He's ready to cum, as he pulls out and quickly moves to her face. Then grabbing head by her hair, he lifts her face and rams his throbbing cock deep into throat. Then with a few thrusts, deep into the back of her throat, gagging her each time. His hot cum begins to spurt, shooting right down her throat. As he shakes and groans with pure satisfaction.

"Swallow it, swallow all of me."

He says as the last few drops shoot out of him.

Then pulling out, he leans down and kisses her forehead.

She's still out of breath as she slowly gets up. Her legs are like jello as she tries

to stand.

He grabs on to her.

"Are you okay?"

He says looking into her eyes.

She smiles.

 "I'm good, great actually."

He grins and raises his eyes brows, with a look of pride.

"That's good to know."

Then he puts his pants back on and hands her, her clothes.

As she puts her clothes back on, she looks at the clock.

"It's getting late, I guess I should get going."

He leans in and kisses her cheek and winks.

"You can cover for your little sister, any time."

She smiles.

"I'll keep that in mind."

Then with one last kiss and sensual wink, she heads out.

While She Sleeps

He lays there, in the darkness of their room. Her laying along side him, sleeping as the moon shines on her face through the window.

The passion in their marriage, long gone. Now just two people together, simply honouring the promise they made.

There is no romance, never and I love you, or sensual glance. They barely speak, other then to say hello or good-bye. His body aches to be touched. His sexual urges nag at him, stroking himself in the shower, is no longer enough. He needs more, he needs passion. He needs to feel himself deep inside a woman.

Then as he lay there, he sees her as she walks past their room. In nothing but her bra and panties. She looks in, knowing he can see her and gives him an inviting look. Her room just down the hall. She's his wife's sister, she had moved in months ago and ever since. She'd been watching him, giving him seductive glares, always leaning over in front of him when ever she had the chance. Enticing him with her cleavage or her tight little ass. He'd wanted her for so long.

Wanted to feel himself deep inside of her, but afraid to make his move. What if she didn't want him too? What if she went to his wife and told her what he'd done.

He couldn't take the risk not knowing, but his body ached. He reached

into his shorts, rubbing his cock. Never enough, he wanted more. When

he looked up, to see her once again at their door.

She winked at him, blew a kiss with her lips and signalled for him to follow.

He could barely contain himself, as he slowly slid out of bed, leaving

his wife to sleep alone and followed her down the hall.

He knocks gently on her door, she opens it. Standing before he him, in her

bright red lace panties and bra.

"It's about time you joined me."

She said, leading him into her room.

"I've wanted you for months, but you never seem to notice."

She says as she reaches into his shorts and takes his now hard cock into her

hand.

Still shocked, yet completely aroused. He pulls her to him, unlatches

bra and slowly takes it off. Then leans in kissing her neck and collar

bone while reaching down to slide off her panties.

She's stroking his cock up and down, making him so hard he can barely take

it. He grabs her pussy and shoves his fingers deep inside of her. Then pulling

them out, he licks them.

Watching him lick her from his fingers, gets her hotter as she bites her lip and

moans.

"Mhmm I want you Sir! Take me, take all of me, I'm yours."

He lifts her up and carries her to the bed. His cock hard and pulsing, wanting

her.

Then laying her on the bed, he climbs over her, straddling her

backwards with his cock just above her mouth.

She licks the tip teasing him, as he pushes down forcing himself into her mouth and begins stroking himself in and out. She's rubbing his balls and teasing his cock with her tongue as he pulls out and pushes back in, deep into the back of her throat.

All the while, he's face down in her pussy. Spreading her lips apart and driving his tongue deep inside of her. Tasting her as the hot juices of her desire flow filling her up and dripping soaking his face.

He begins pushing himself faster and faster deep into her mouth. Then just as he feels, he's about to cum. He pulls out, quickly turns around and rams his cock deep into her pussy.

So deep he can't go any further. He's all the way inside of her. Pounding her hard, she starts to scream as she pulls the pillow over her face to muffle the sounds. She's gripping it hard, moaning and screaming. He pounds her over and over.

Ramming her so hard she can barely take it.

"That's a good girl, take it, take all of it!"

He groans as he pushes so hard and deep her legs are forced further apart.

She cries out

"I'm your's Master! I'm yours!"

He moans and grunts, his body shaking as he rams himself in and out of her. Her body now convulsing as she starts to cum all over his cock. Feeling her warm cum, coating his cock deep inside of her, sends waves coursing through his body as he moans and begins to twitch shooting his hot cum deep inside of her.

Then pulling out, he lays next to her on the bed.

"I want to feel guilty, but I don't."

He says looking up at the ceiling.

She kisses his cheek.

"Then don't, Master"

Then getting up from the bed, she looks to him.

"I'm yours whenever you want me."

She's says.

He smiles and slaps her ass. Then slips back into his shorts and with one last kiss. Creeps back down the hall and slips into bed, next to his wife.

Wake up call

Sliding in to bed next to her, curled up hugging her pillow. Her hair a mess, covering her face.

The moonlight bouncing off her naked shoulders.

The sight of her, laying there. Completely naked and vulnerable, turned him on. As he lay there, watching her sleep, he grabs on to his cock and starts stroking it. He wants her, he wants her bad, but she lay there asleep. Did he dare wake her? He continued stroking himself, his cock rock hard. His body needing her. He rolls over and spoons her, with his hard cock pressed against her ass. He starts pushing himself against her harder, hoping to wake her, but she doesn't move.

He reaches around and caresses her pussy, slowly slipping his fingers inside of her. She moans as she starts to wake and parts her legs for him. He fingers her harder and faster. Her pussy getting wetter and wetter as his kisses the back of her neck and moans in her ear.

Getting turned on, she starts to squirm and arches her back into him. With his other hand her grabs her breast. Her nipples now hard, her body wanting him.

He squeezes them hard, she moans and pushes her ass hard against him. He starts fingering her pussy faster and faster, now soaked and ready for his cock.

Her eyes barely open, still sleepy. She reaches behind her and grabs his hard cock in her hand and starts stroking it.

"Mmhm you're so hard."

She moans, stroking him faster.

Her pussy throbbing, soaked and dripping as his fingers ram in and out of her. Her body quivering, moans now shooting from her throat involuntarily. Her body now his, as she starts to shake and erotic pulsations shoot through pussy, she starts moaning louder, grabbing his cock harder as she bursts and her cum shoots all over his fingers.

Then pulling them out, he licks them clean and reaches down to slide his rock hard cock into her soaked pussy, taking her from behind.

He pushes himself inside of her, she pushes against him forcing him deeper. Now all inside of her, he starts pushing himself in and out of her. Slow, then fast, then slow again. Pulling almost all the way at times to tease her, before ramming it back in hard and deep.

She grabs on to her breasts and starts squeezing them and playing with her nipples. Him lost in the moment, grabs on to her shoulder with his mouth bites her hard. It hurts and she lets out a painful cry. He moves to her neck, he kisses it and sucks it, leaving behind yet another love bite. He's now so hard and deep inside of her, his cock throbs. He starts pounding her harder and harder, pushing deeper each time. Her moans now turned to cries of pain, but she doesn't I stop him. She grips on to the pillow even biting it to drown out the sounds of her cries. Seeing this, he starts moving even faster, in and out of her. His body shaking, his cock throbbing and ready to blow.

He grabs her tight,

"That's my girl, take it. You like it don't you? Tell me, tell me you like it!"

She moans, tears now involuntarily streaming from her eyes.

"Yes Master, I like it. I'm yours all yours."

Hearing her reply sends a shiver through his body.

Now ready to cum, his body twitches and shakes. He moans as his thrusts slow with his impending orgasm. Then with one final ram of his cock, so deep he hits the back of her pussy he blows his load deep inside of her.

Then as they lay there, his cock still inside of her.

He whispers.

"Are you still tired?"

She moans turning her head towards him.

"Mmhmm I'm awake now!"

He tilts her head back and kisses her on the lips.

"Good, because I'm not finished yet!"

Then pulling out he smacks her ass.

"Come on, you've got some work to do!"

He says laying on his back on the bed.

Knowing exactly what he wants, she gets on her knees and moves towards him. She starts running her long nails up and down his body, then grabbing his inner thigh she starts to squeeze and massage it, while leaning in and running her tongue up and down his cock.

Now starting to awaken again. She licks his balls and runs her tongue all the way down, nearly to his ass. He shivers as she hits his spot, the spot that makes him go wild.

Then moving up, she starts to suck on his cock. Pushing him in and out of her mouth, stopping at the tip to tease him, then pushing back deep into her throat. With each stroke, his cock gets harder and his body ready for more.

He reaches behind her, grabs her ass and slides his fingers into her pussy, getting them nice and wet. Then pulling out, he moves to her ass and starts fingering it. Pushing his finger deep inside, getting her ready for him.

She's moaning, and squirming, while still pushing his cock deep into mouth. Now rock hard again, it gags her as it hits the back of her throat.

He slaps her ass as he pulls away and gets up on his knees.

" Get in front of me, on your knees. Ass up face down."

He demands.

She moves quickly, her ass now facing him as he moves in.

He pushes his fingers inside of her pussy then wipes them on her ass. Then parting her legs just enough, he starts to push his hard cock into her ass. Slowly pushing it inside of her, she screams and groans as he gets the tip inside. It hurts, he's holding her, keeping her from pulling away as he pushes harder and harder. Now almost all the way in, he whispers.

"Are you ready? I'm going in all the way now."

She moans as she replies.

"Yes Sir, do it. Take me!"

Then with one hard push he rammed himself deep inside of her. His cock filling her ass, so tight and so deep. It hurt, she cried out with screams of pain as he started pounding her over and over. So hard she could no longer control the sounds shooting from her throat.

She grabbed into the sheets so hard, she nearly tore them off the bed. He grabbed her hand holding it as she squeezed it so hard it turned him on even more and he began pounding her ass even harder. Then slipping his finger into her mouth, she starting sucking on it, still moaning and trying not to scream. She sucked his finger pushing it in and out of her mouth. His body now jerking with pleasure groans shooting from his throat, she knows he's about to cum as she screams out.

"Oh yea, cum for me Master! Cum deep inside of my ass."

Then with a loud grunt and hard ram into her ass. His body starts to shake, as his hot cum flows and fills her ass to the brim. Then after a few more small pushes, he pulls out and lays on the bed next to her. Her ass and pussy, both now soaked and dripping from cum.

"How's that for a wake up call?"

He says to her, as she gets up to clean herself up.

She smiles and raises her eyebrows as she replies.

"Couldn't possibly think of a better way to waken."

He reaches over and smacks her ass.

"That's my girl!"

Back Road Rendezvous

Headlights beaming outside her window and pulling into her driveway. Her heart started pounding, he was here. She'd been waiting for felt like forever, to be alone with him. She nervously grabbed her purse and ran out to meet him. Then jumping into his truck next to him, they were off.

As they pulled around the corner and away from her house, he leaned over and kissed her.

"Does he know where you went?"

He asked.

She was married yet separated, still living in the same house.

"No he didn't ask, so I never said."

She answered, as he reached down took her hand in his.

They drove for a bit, talking about each of their lives and how so many things had changed. They were loves from the past, still carrying a torch for each other. Now reunited and connected as if they'd never been apart.

Their relationship a secret from both her family and his. The only way to be together, was to sneak away to be alone. Their love now a back road rendezvous, as parking on dark back roads, was their only place to be completely alone.

He pulled down a dark dirt road, driving far enough down that he was unseen from the busy street ahead. Then pulled off to the side and parked.

Then leaning over, he grabbed her head pulled her to him and kissed her.

His cock getting hard in jeans, wanting her, wanting to feel her mouth wrapped tightly around him. He unzips his jeans and pulls out his cock. Then pushing her head downward, he says.

"Why don't you re-introduce yourself"

She moans as she leans down taking him into her mouth. Slowly sucking on him, pushing him in and out her mouth. While reaching in and stroking his balls with her hand.

His cock getting harder as he starts pushing, forcing himself deeper into her mouth, hitting the back of her throat, she gags. Then sliding up to the tip, she pops off and teases the tip with her tongue, while stroking him hard and fast with her hand.

He pushes her head forcing her to take him back into her mouth.

"Suck it, take all of it."

He says forcing himself deeper, while reaching into her pants and squeezing her ass.

She moans sucking him faster and faster, gagging herself with the tip of his cock. Hearing the gagging sounds coming from

Her throat, brought out the animal him. Now taking over, pushing himself, hard and deep into her throat. Grunting and moaning while holding her head so couldn't pull away.

"Ah that's my girl! Take that, take it!"

He groans as he's about ready to cum. Then stopping himself he pulls out and gets on his knees and lays her back. Then quickly pulling down her pants and putting her legs up on his shoulders, he drives his cock hard and deep into her pussy. Pounding her over and over, her head hitting the window, he takes his shirt and tucks it in behind her. He's so deep inside of her, it hurts but at the same time she likes it.

He continues pounding her in and out, fast, then slow then fast again. He reaches down and encircles her clit with his thumb. Her body tingling, the passion taking over as she screams and squirms below him. Her body completely his, she feels herself ready to cum.

Him feeling her becoming wetter and wetter, his cock soaked inside of her, moans.

"You're so wet, cum for me, cum for me now!" He demands.

"Who owns you, who owns this pussy?"

Him still pounding her so hard, it's hard to catch her breath, as she answers.

" You do Sir, you do."

Then the waves of erotic pleasure take over and she burst into massive orgasm and the sounds of pleasure shoot from her throat.

He leaned down and kissed her as he whispered.

"It's Daddy's turn now! On your knees, turn around. I'm going to pound your ass now."

She turned around, nervous. She had never done anal before, but she loved him and wanted nothing more then to please him. Her body was completely in his control.

He leaned her further forward and pulled her ass closer to him. Then reaching into her pussy, he used her own cum, to wet her ass. Then pushed his fingers into ass getting her ready for him. Her heart was pounding, she was shaking, as he started to push himself inside of her. It hurt, she unintentionally pulled forward. He grabbed her hips pulling her back to him.

"Don't pull away."

He demanded

"Once the tip is in, it will be easier."

Then pushing harder, he forced himself further inside of her. Still not all the way in, her eyes are tearing. It hurts, it burns, but she's doesn't stop him. Then finally he rams himself hard, shoving his cock all the way into her ass. She let out a loud scream of pain, it hurt like nothing she'd felt before, yet at the same time she wanted him to continue. She gripped on to the door of his truck, tears now streaming down her face. Cries of pain shooting from her throat. As he pounded her ass harder and harder filling her with rock hard throbbing cock. Hearing her cries turned him on and he started pounding even harder, loud grunts and groans now coming from him as he's getting close to cumming.

"I'm going to fill your ass with my cum. Are you ready for it? Tell me are you?"

He grunted while driving himself in and out.

Her unable to even catch her breath answered.

"Yes Master, yes!"

Hearing her call him Master, aroused him further. As his body began to convulse and his hot cum shot deep into her ass. Filling her so full, that it dripped from her when he pulled out. Her ass hurt, but she said nothing. He had no idea, that she had never done anal before and she never wanted to tell him. Pleasing him was what she wanted most.

Then as she turned over, to put her pants back on.

He leaned over and kissed her,

"I love you."

She looked into his eyes and replied.

"I love you too."

Then with that, he drove her back home, until next time.

Truck stop cutie

There she was, once again sitting alone in truck stop diner. He'd been through there, every week for months and every time there she was. A cute little brunette, with a sweet face and the most beautiful eyes he'd ever seen. He'd never seen her with anyone, she was always on her own.

Every week, he'd wanted to speak to her but wasn't sure how to approach her, without scaring her off.

He couldn't help but watch her, something about her just drew his eyes to her. Time and time again, he watched her from a far, intrigued by her and wondering what it was that, brought her to sit in a truck stop diner each and every week.

Then as he sat, drinking his coffee and staring in her direction, she looked up. Then from across the room, for the first time their eyes met.

He gave her a nod and a wink, she smiled and blushed, looking back down at the table.

Then calling his waitress over, he pointed to her and offered to pay for her order. Then he watched as the waitress walked over to tell her.

She was grateful as she looked up and smiled at him, then getting up from her table walked over to him.

"Can I join you?"

She asked.

He smirked.

" You sure can, have a seat!"

"I see you here every week, you must like it here."

He said as she sat down next to him.

"To be honest, I do. My father was a trucker, so I grew up around Truckers and since my Father passed. I come here once a week, it kind of feels like home." She said looking him in the eyes.

He reached putting his hand on her shoulder.

"I see, I'm sorry for your loss. So I guess being around us Truckers makes you feel close to your father then?"

She sighed as she replied.

"Yes, some what. I also just love trucking in general though and I know how lonely you boys can get out on the road."

He raised his eyebrows and grinned, unsure where all of this was headed.

   She put her hand under the table and squeezed his thigh, as she slid closer to him.

" can we go to your truck?"

She asked.

She was so very beautiful, but also so young. He wanted her, but was it the right thing to do.

" darlin' I'm old enough to be your father. What do you want with an old man like me?"

He said, putting his hand on hers.

She leaned over and whispered in his ear.

"The older the better, honey!"

Clearly she was a girl with Daddy issues, having lost her trucker father.

"Sweetie, are you sure that is really what you want?"

He said running his hand up her arm.

Under the table, she ran her hand up his thigh to bulge now in his pants.

"Oh I'm sure, don't you want me too?"

She said as she started rubbing him, making him harder.

She was so sweet and appeared so innocent, yet clearly she was not. Reaching under the table, he grabbed her hand and pushed it off of him.

"Okay, if you're coming to my truck, you better stop that or I won't be able to get up!"

She giggled and gave him a seductive look, licking her lips with her tongue.

Then sliding out of the booth, they headed out to his truck. He helped her up into the truck, her tight little ass right there in front of him, already turning him on.

"Welcome to my home on the road"

He said, as she made herself comfortable.

Then moving towards him, she started unbuttoning his shirt. She wasn't wasting any time.

"Do you want me Daddy?"

She said slowly kissing his chest.

He slid his hand up her shirt and started rubbing her breasts. Her nipples now hard, he grabbed on pinching them hard. She stopped and removed her shirt, then standing there topless before him, she whispered.

"I'm yours Daddy, take me!"

Becoming aroused.

He ripped down her pants and started rubbing her pussy, then leaning in he kissed it and ran his tongue across.

She moaned.

"Tell me what you want Daddy, I'm all yours."

She said looking into his eyes.

Hearing her words turned him on releasing his animal ways.

"Suck my cock my little slut!"

He said grabbing her and pushing her head towards the bulge in his pants.

Unzipping his pants, she took his hard cock into her hand and started stroking it.

Then pushing it into her mouth she started to suck him, while stroking him at the same time.

He'd been on the road for months, alone and untouched by anyone. His body now so aroused he became out of control. He pushed her head hard onto his cock and held it there. As he took over, ramming his cock deep into her throat. Gagging her so hard, her eyes teared and her face covered in steaks from her running mascara. He pushed hard, faster and faster, his body shaking with the pleasure from the tip of his cock, hitting the back of her throat. The sounds of her gagging turning him on further, but not wanting to cum yet. He yanked her head off of him and demanded.

"Get on the bed, ass up. I want to pound your tight little ass!"

She moaned getting on the bed.

" Yes Daddy."

There on her knees, ass in the air. He came up behind her. Her ass was dry, but he didn't care. He pulled her closer to him. Spread her ass cheeks and rammed his cock inside of her. He never took it slow, just rammed her hard. His animal nature had taken over and he just let her have it, hard and deep. She screamed with pain as he pounded her over and over, holding on her hips keeping her from pulling away from him. She put her head down in the pillow, he grabbed her hair pulling it back up.

"Take it, take it my little slut."

He said pounding her so hard, sounds of pain were being forced from her throat.

She cried out

"Give it to me Daddy, yes punish me Daddy, punish me."

Her face soaked with tears, her voice throaty from screaming so loudly. He continued to ram himself in and out of her. She gripped the bed sheets so tightly her hands were almost numb. Her ass hurt, it was on fire from his huge cock pounding her so hard, but she never stopped him. He smacked her ass hard as his body began to shake.

"That's Daddy's girl, take it take it all."

His body now jerking groans shooting from his throat as he's about to cum. Then pulling out of her ass, he strokes himself finishing off across her ass. His hot cum, shooting out of him right across her ass and on to her back.

Then smacking her ass and getting up, he tosses her a towel and says.

"Here, clean yourself up!"

She smiles at him and winks

"Yes Daddy!"

Room with a view

Standing in front of her window, she watched him. Tall, tanned a six pack and an ass that would drive any woman wild. She tried not to watch, but the sight of him drew her in every time. She was in the room across the way, her window looking right across into his. Every day she would see him, she never knew his name or anything about him, other then the fact that seeing him, turned her on in way that was wild and intense.

As she stood watching, she saw him walk over to his door, opening it. There stood a woman. A beautiful woman, long blonde hair all the way down to her perfect little ass. Big breasts bulging from the top of her skimpy little tank top. Was this a girlfriend, or a call girl? Not knowing intrigued her as she watched them. He led her into his room, pulled her to him, grabbed her face and kissed her long and passionately, burying his tongue deep in her throat. Then leaning down, he licked the top of her breasts, popping out of her top.

Across the way she watched them. She knew it was wrong, but she couldn't look away.

He slid his hand into her pants, right into her silky lace panties and started fingering her tight little pussy. She leaned in to him, her body body melting into his. As he then slid her pants all the way down and scooped her up carrying her to his bed. Then taking his cloths off, he got on to the bed. Spread her legs wide and got down to eat her out. Burying his face into her pussy, he started licking her, slowly then faster and faster then slow again teasing her with his tongue, then burying it deep inside of her to taste her. She moaned and squirmed as he continued going at her licking her, now pushing his fingers deep inside of her and even knuckling her now soaked pussy and fingering her ass. Then putting her legs up his shoulders, he pushes his fingers deeper inside of her harder and faster while licking her clit with his tongue. She's moaning and shrieking with pleasure, her body completely overcome as her pussy squirts right in his face. He keeps going at her, faster and faster.

"Cum my dirty little slut, cum!"

He blurts out while smacking her pussy and she squirts again.

She's writhing about, he's holding her down while he continues to lick her and even bites her.

Across the way, still watching. She's getting hot, as she reaches into her panties and fingers herself while watching them.

He continues licking her ferociously ramming his fingers deep inside of her. Her body now shaking, she's panting and moaning as she loses all control of her senses and screams out.

"I'm cumming, I'm cumming ahhh ahhh!"

He pushes his tongue deep inside of her and tastes her, while she cums all over his face. Then slapping her thigh, he gets up.

"Move up on the bed."

He demands, and she slides up. He goes to the bedside table, opens the drawer and pulls out handcuffs and a vibrator. Then moving back to the bed, he handcuffs her hands to the headboard. Then moving down and using two of his neck ties, he spreads her legs wide snd ties her legs to the footboard.

Now she lay there, tied up, spread eagle. All his, to do with as he wished. Watching through the window, seeing the other woman tied up, like his sexy little prisoner, turned her on. Her pussy soaked and throbbing as she moves her fingers in and out, encircling her clit with her finger tips and even fingering own ass. She, continued watching waiting for what was next.

He grabbed the vibrator and moved towards her. Turning it on, he slowly slid it up and down her body, circling her nipples, now so hard they ached. She wanted him inside of her, her pussy throbbed aching for his cock.

He moved the vibrator down, slowly moving it across her pussy and enticing her as it rolled over her hard clit. She squirmed her body all his. Her pussy so wet it dripped. He continued teasing her, her body quivering and jerking from pleasure. Her pussy tingling, her orgasm building as she moaned and panted loudly. The vibrations causing pulsations shooting through her body, she starts to scream as her pussy bursts into massive orgasm.

Her body convulsing, on the bed the pleasure almost more then she can take, as he keeps going. Stroking the vibrator up and down her body and across her now over stimulated pussy. She wants him, she wants him inside of her as she screams out.

"Pound my pussy, pound it please!"

He continues with the vibrator as she squirms.

"Beg me, beg for me my little whore!"

He shouts out.

"Who's your Master?"

He asks, leaning down and biting her breast hard leaving behind his teeth marks. It hurt, she jerked as she screamed.

"You are, you're my Master! Please Master, please pound my pussy!"

Tossing the vibrator aside, he untied her legs and took off the hand cuffs. Then

sliding in between her legs. He smacked her thigh.

"Roll over, on your knees."

She rolled over and he came up behind her. Her pussy soaked as he drove himself

deep inside of her hard. So hard he hit the back the wall, forcing a scream of pain

to shoot from her throat.

"You want it? You want it hard don't you?"

He asked leaning down and biting her ass then continuing to drive his cock inside

of her.

Cries of pain echoed thorough the room as she replied trying to catch her breath.

"Yes Master yes, I want it hard. Give it to me Master, give it to me."

He rammed his cock harder and harder inside her. Now almost numb from the pain,

she bit on to the pillows trying to hang on.

   Then right as she thought, she couldn't take anymore he pulled out, not yet

finished though, he moved to her ass.

   Then spreading her ass cheeks apart, he spit on her getting it wetter and started

to slide his cock inside of her. He pushed in just the tip, she screamed as the

feeling of his swollen cock burned and hurt. He pulled her closer to him.

"Hang on, I'm going all the way in."

He said, as he pushed hard and forced himself all the way into her ass. She let out

a loud scream of pain, her scream turning him wild as he began pounding her

harder and harder. Not even giving her time to breath. So deep inside of her, she

felt like her body was no longer hers. She hurt so bad but couldn't stop him, she

was his and he was in control.

Pounding her over and over with no break in his thrusts. His body slapping hard

against her ass. Tears streaming down her face, her knuckles white, gripping so tightly on to the sheets. Now screaming so loudly, that he reaches around and covers her mouth with his hand. Then taking his finger into her mouth, she starts to suck it. Feeling this, his body starts to shake. He lets out a loud groan, then moans as his thrusts start to slow and his cock begins to pulse. Then with one final deep ram into her ass, he cums. Filling her ass so full, that his cum dripped from her when he pulled out.

  Across the way, watching them. She continued fingering her pussy until she cummed all over herself. She had gotten so hot and so turned on by them, it was as if she were right there with them.

   He got up from the bed, she lay there almost motionless, trying catch her breath. He picked up her clothes and tossed them to her, then handed her a towel.

"Clean yourself up and get dressed."

He demanded, as she slowly got up.

Then handing her some cash, he leaned down and kissed the top of her head.

"I'm going to the shower, show yourself out. I'll see you next week."

He said, as he walked away. She got dressed and left.

Across the way, she watched as the women who clearly had been a call girl left, his room.

Meet me at Route 69

Rolling on the down the highway, nothing but taillights ahead and the moon lighting up the night sky. Headed for the Route 69 truck stop, where his girl waited for him.

They always spent months apart, him always on the road and her so busy in her own life. Getting away with him was always too difficult.

The route 69 truck stop, had quickly become their place. They would meet up there, when ever he was headed through and finally get their time alone together.

Only a few miles left to go, he was anxious to see her again. She waited for him, she had missed him for so long, she couldn't wait be with him.

Her phone buzzed, looking down it was a message from him, that read.

"Five minutes away"

Her heart started to pound in her chest as she anxiously waited for his truck to roll in, then as she looked up, there he was pulling in. She waited for him to park, then headed over to his truck. He climbed out and walked over to her. She grabbed him and planted a great big kiss right on his lips.

"Mmhmm that's the stuff!"

She said, then wrapping her arms around him and hugging him.

Once in truck, there was no time wasted. He pulled her close to him and grabbed her breasts, squeezing her nipples through her shirt.

"Is that a bra? You know better then to wear a bra when you meet up with me."

He said, reaching down and squeezing her ass hard.

She unlatched her bra and removed it, dropping it on the floor.

"There you go, problem solved."

She said, leaning in and kissing his neck and running her tongue up to his ear.

He shivered, grabbing her shirt and pulling it off. Then leaning down to bite her breast, biting it so hard he left behind a bruise of his teeth marks.

Then taking his shirt off, he pulled her against him. Her hard nipples pressed against his bare chest. He kissed her neck and sucked on it, leaving behind yet another love bite.

" take off your pants and get on the bed."

He demanded.

She moaned.

"Mmhmm yes Sir."

Then slipping out of her pants, she slid on to his bed and he crawled in beside her. Both of them naked, their bodies pressed together.

She kissed him, he kissed her back. Then looking into eyes, he says.

"You know what to do."

She moans, as she starts running her nails and her tongue all the way down his body. Teasing him, making him shiver with her touch.

She moves slowly towards his hard cock. She grabs it, stroking it and running her nails all the way down to a spot that drives him wild. He jerks and shivers as she sends sensations shooting through his body.

Then taking him into her mouth, she starts sucking his cock while still stroking his balls with her hand. She pushes him in and out of her mouth, fast then slow then fast again. Stopping to lick the tip, teasing him, then pushing it back into her mouth. He pushing up, forcing himself deeper into her mouth, then pushing her head forcing himself into her throat. She gags and her eyes water as she moves faster and faster, sucking him and teasing him with her tongue. While continuing to run her nails down to his spot causing him to jerk each time she hits it. He's becoming wildly turned on, his inner animal now unleashed as he pulls out of her mouth and moves in front of her.

"Lay down"

He says smacking her thigh, then leaning in and biting her again, this time on her collar bone.

She lay back and he quickly pulled her to him. Ramming his cock deep into her soaked pussy.

"Mmhmm you're so wet, I like it."

He says, ramming himself deeper inside of her.

He's so deep it hurts, then right when she thinks, he couldn't possibly go deeper. He rams himself even further. Moans forced from her throat with each thrust. So deep inside of her, her legs forced further apart. He pounded her harder and harder, he grabbed her breasts squeezing them and twisting her nipples.

He grabs her pussy while still pounding it.

"Who's pussy is this? Tell me? Who's?"

He asks while staring deep into her eyes.

Moans still being forced from her throat. Almost hard to speak she answers.

"Yours Master, yours."

He continues pounding her pussy, now so soaked it drips. Her body beginning to shake, as the sensation of her arising orgasm takes over. Her pussy heating up, pulsations taking over. She moans louder and pants unable to catch her breath as she cums all over his cock deep inside of her.

"That's my girl."

He says, tapping her thigh.

"Now roll over, so I can finish up."

She rolls over and he comes up behind her.

Then using her cum, to wet her ass he starts pushing himself inside. Barely inside, she screams and pulls away. He grabs her pulling her hard to him.

"Don't pull away, let it happen or it will hurt worse."

Tears now in her eyes, she hung on and he quickly rammed himself deep into her ass.

She grabbed on to the pillows tight, pushing her face into them, trying to muffle the sounds of her cries. He pushed faster and faster, harder each time. Her ass filled by his swollen rock hard cock. She's screaming into the pillows, a sound that sends him wild as he rams her deeper and harder, holding her tight so she can't pull away. His body out of his control, waves of pleasure coursing through him. He groans loud and with one more hard thrust he rams himself deeper as he cums filling her ass right up, with his hot cum.

Then leaning down he kisses the back of her neck.

"Wow I missed you."

He whispered.

Then pulling out, he lays down beside her.

She leans over and kissed him.

"I missed you too, I love you."

He kisses her back.

"I love you too."

Then as they lay there together, she rubs his body. Massaging his muscles, completely relaxing him. She rubbed his back, then his legs, even his ass. Then as she lay there beside him, they fell fast asleep in each other's arms.

Tag Team

Friends with benefits, their relationship open and free of commitment. Each of them free to do as they pleased. Getting together, when ever they were free, fulfilling each other's deepest fantasies. At this point, they had pretty much tried it all. All except for one of her fantasies that she had kept to herself, until now. She had always fantasized about being with two men at once, but never had the guts to go for it.

Now tonight, he had invited one of his friends to join them and make her fantasy a reality.

She was nervous, yet at the same time excited as she sat with him, anxiously awaiting his friends arrival.

"Are you nervous?"

He asked putting his hand on her thigh

She shrugged her shoulders.

"Maybe a little, I guess."

Then moving over and straddling his lap, she said.

"I know how we could kill some time."

He moaned.

"Mmhm me too."

He said, smacking her ass.

nches her fists. The other guy hearing the sounds shooting from her throat,

es wild now ramming her mouth so hard, her gagging muffled the sounds. Both

en pounding her hard and deep, she can barely catch her breath in between

gging and the cries of pain. Then just as her friend's about the cum, he pulls

nself out of her pussy and shoots his hot cum all across her ass. The other guy

eing this and ready to cum himself. Pulls out of her mouth and then stroking

nself. He shoots his cum all over her face.

Then as she lay there, naked and covered in their cum, he leans down and

ses the top of her head and her friend kisses her lips.

"Are you okay?"

r friend asks.

e moans and kisses him back.

n great, going to grab a shower though."

e said getting up from the floor.

smacks her ass.

kay, make it a quick one. It's Friday night, we'll watch a movie."

e laughs

unds good"

she headed into the shower waving good bye to his friend.

moaning as her ass is pounded hard and deep, over and over. Two cocks

pounding her, one in her ass one in her mouth. She reaches between her

and starts playing with her own pussy, encircling her clit with her fingertips

both men continue pushing their cocks in and out of her. Her body begins

shake, she moans loud. Her pussy tingling and ready to cum. Both men he

her moans of pleasure ready to cum themselves.

Then as her pussy starts to cum, her body shakes involuntarily and pulsat

shoot through her ass tightening around his cock, driving him wild and brir

him go cum deep inside of her ass. Her friend hearing the sounds of them

Cumming together, begins to shake and groan as he joins them and shoo

load right down her throat and she swallows every drop.

Then switching it up, she turns around with her pussy just above her frien

and her right in front of the other guys cock. She opens her mouth and tal

inside starts to suck while rubbing his balls, getting him hard again. While

friend reaches up and buries his face in her pussy. Licking and teasing it

tongue and shoving his fingers deep inside. She's so wet she drips on hi:

His cock now rock hard again as the taste her sends him wild. Now push

fingers fast in and out of her, her body squirming above him. She's moar

body filled with intense pleasure.

The other guy now ramming his cock in and out of her mouth. Driving it

and deep her eyes water and her black mascara steaks her face.

Her friend, now so hard he's ready to explode. Slides out from und

and gets up behind, then moving his cock to her pussy, he drives it in h

deep. So deep it hurt as she involuntarily pulled away. He grabs her hi

her back. Ramming himself hard in and and out of her. Her pussy drip

cock throbbing inside of her. Now pounding her so hard. She cries out

Daddy's girl

Coming in from work, he sees her. She's sitting there on the sofa, quietly reading a book. Just as always, wearing nothing but her skimpy little shorts with her ass cheeks hanging out the bottom and cut off tank top, so tight the top of her breasts pop out the top. Enticing him, every chance she got. A beautiful young girl, barely twenty one. His step daughter and also his biggest temptation. A real Daddy's girl, they had always been close, but as she got older their relationship was becoming something more. A forbidden love aching to break free. Every day she flirted with him, bending over in front of him with her ass nearly in his face and leaning forward so he could see right down her top. He had grown to want her in an a way that a father shouldn't be wanting his daughter. Even though a step daughter, he had still raised her as his own. Her flirtatious ways however brought out a side of him that was almost unnatural. She made it appear more and more obvious by the day that she wanted him too.

He walked into the living room, putting his hand on her shoulder, he asked.

"How was you day?"

She shrugged her shoulders.

" Ahh it was okay I guess. Kind of boring, not much happening"

He sat down beside her on the sofa, to his surprise she slid closer to him.

"Mom called earlier, she's working late tonight. Just us for dinner I guess."

He put his hand on her thigh.

"Mmhmm yea I'm great too. A little shocked with did this, but great."

She laughed.

"Ahh yea, no worries Daddy. You'll get used to it!"

She said, as she kissed his cheek.

Then headed to the shower, she looked back.

"You can order the pizza now, I'm famished."

Call Me Madam

What makes you think, you're suitable to move into the house?

She asked, walking around her chair checking her out.

Looking up at her, almost stuttering she replied.

"Well Ma'am"

She stopped her, blurting out.

"Call me Madam!"

She continued.

"I'm sorry Madam, I'm young, I'm fit and I'm open to trying anything."

Madam raised her eyebrows asking her to get up.

"Well get up, let's take a look at you then."

She stood up, her perky breasts popping out of the top of her slightly

unbuttoned shirt. Her tiny little waist in her skin tight jeans.

"Hmm Not bad."

Madam, said while continuing to check her out.

"So let me ask you. Will you do anal? Do you deep throat? Will you be a

submissive if that's what the gentleman wants? Or visa versa, will you

command him? Is there anything you won't do?"

Wanting to please Madam, she anxiously answered.

"Oh yes, I'll do it all and have, there's really nothing I won't do. I'm sure there won't be any disappointed clients."

Madam raised her eyebrows and nodded.

"Hmm I see! Well okay then, I give you trial."

She looked up to her.

"A trial?"

Madam continued.

"Yes, I have a client who likes to be controlled. You'll have to demand everything from him, make him your submissive. If you can please him without a complaint. You're in, you can move in and work for me here in the house."

She smiled as she got up from her chair.

"Thank you Madam, I'm sure there won't be any complaints. Thank you for giving me a chance. "

Madam reached out handing her a room key.

"You can go up to this room, there's outfits and everything you need in there. Have yourself ready to meet him in an hour."

She headed up to the room, the entire room done in black and red satin and lace. She went to the closet, where she found a black leather corset, crotchless panties and thigh high fish net stockings and on the closet door hung a whip.

She slipped out of her clothes, then putting on the leather corset, panties and stockings. Then slipping into some black stilettos, she was ready for him.

She drew the curtains making the room dark and turned on a dim red light above the bed. Then pulled out the whip and waited for him to arrive.

A knock on the door, her heart started pounding as she called out.

"Come in."

It was Madam checking up on her.

"You look ready are you? He's downstairs."

She quickly answered.

"Yes I'm ready, send him up."

Madam left and moments later, another knock

on the door. Knowing it was him,

she demanded.

"Come in and get on your knees, bow to me and kiss my feet."

Dropping to his knees, he bowed, then crawling to her, he kissed her feet.

"Now up on your feet"

She commanded, slapping the whip across the back of a chair.

He quickly jumped up, standing before her.

"Take off your clothes."

She instructed, as she stood watching him.

"Yes Ma'am"

he answered looking down at her feet, while starting to remove his clothes.

"Hurry up!"

She shouted at him, while cracking the whip again.

He sped up, quickly removing his clothes and standing naked before her.

Then resting the whip on his shoulder, she slowly circled him, checking him out.

"Not bad. Not bad at all."

She said, then commanded him down on his knees.

Quickly falling to his knees he looked up at her.

She grabbed him by the hair and pushed his face against her pussy.

"Eat my pussy, eat it good and don't stop until I cum all over your face."

She demanded.

He moaned heeding her commands as he started licking and nibbling at her pussy.

Pushing his tongue deep inside of her. His cock now rock hard, turned on by her every move.

He licked her faster and faster, her pussy wet and starting to drip on his face. His fingers deep inside of her, sliding in and out fast then slow then fast again.

"Make me cum!"

She commanded,

as he pushed his tongue deep inside of her, tasting her sweet pussy.

Her body shaking, her pussy ready to cum. She grabs his head pushing it harder against her.

"That's it, good boy! Make my pussy cum."

He licked her faster and faster, her body shaking with sheer satisfaction as she involuntarily squirted all over his face.

Never skipping a beat, he continued to lick

her pussy and drive his tongue deep inside of her bringing her to massive orgasm and her cum dripped from her and on to his face.

"Lick me clean, lick me dry she instructed."

Holding his head against her.

"Yes Ma'am"

He replied as he moaned then licked her pussy and sucked the cum right out of her.

Then cracking the whip on the floor next to him and pulling him up by the hair.

She whispered.

"Now pound my ass with your hard cock and fill me with your cum."

Then bending over in front of him, with her ass in his direction, she shouted.

"Now! Do it now!"

He pulled her ass to him spreading her apart.

 "Yes Ma'am!"

As he pushed his hard cock into her ass. He pushed slowly, little by little like he was afraid to hurt her.

Pushing her ass hard against him, she demanded.

"Harder, push it in there NOW!"

Hearing her commands he rammed himself hard into her ass, it hurt as she let out a scream.

"That's it, hurt me, pound my ass."

She shouted as he started pounding her harder and harder pushing his cock deeper inside of her.

"Pound me, pound me until you cum."

She demanded.

Her demands turning him on as he pushed faster and faster, his body shaking with pleasure with her ass so tight around his cock.

"Cum for me, cum for me now!"

She shouted at him while he continued forcing himself in and out of her and she shrieked with sounds of both pain and pleasure.

His body now shuttering, ready to cum. He's deep inside of her, his thrusts slow, he jerks shooting his cum and filling her ass.

"Good boy, that's it."

She says as he pulls out and stays in his knees .

"Now up on feet, put your clothes back on."

She commanded.

" Yes Ma'am"

he said getting dressed and standing before her.

Resting the whip on his shoulder then pointing towards the door, she said

"Good boy. I think we're done here, you can go now."

Then looking up from the floor, headed to the door without even making eye contact. He says.

" Yes Ma'am, Thank you Ma'am"

Then he leaves.

Shortly there after, another knock on the door. It was Madam.

" Well" she said.

"it seems our client enjoyed his time with you. You can move your things into the house, when ever you're ready."

She was excited, but trying not to appear overly anxious, she smiled, then raising her eyebrows, she replied.

"Thank you Madam, thank you so much. I'll move in right away. You won't be disappointed, I promise."

Madam smiled back.

"I'm going to hold you to that!"

Then winked at her and walked away.

Two For One

Finally the last hour of the day and end of the work week. The weekend seemed to take forever to get there.

Gemma was filing papers, anxious to get out of there and home to relax.

Grabbing a new stack files, she looks to her friend, Jessie, sitting off the side doing paper work.

"Almost time to get out of here, damn it's been a long week!"

"It sure has, I thought it would never end."

said Jessie, looking up from her desk, then asking.

"Am I still coming over tonight?

Looking back from the filing cabinet, Gemma answered.

"I sure hope so!"

"Is Keith coming over too?"

She asked.

Getting up from her desk, to hand Gemma some more files, Jessie looked to see if anyone was watching. Then leaned in, kissed her on the cheek and whispered.

"You bet, he's joining us!"

Gemma smiled and winked back at her.

"Perfect, now just to get the heck out of here,"

"Yea no kidding, only half hour to go now!"

said Jessie returning to her desk.

"I have a quick stop after work, then I'll be right over. I'll be there before Keith for sure."

She said.

"Perfect, gives us some time first then."

Gemma replied, winking at her.

Jessie winked back and giving her a seductive smile replied.

"That's the plan!"

"Now let's get out of here. I'll see you at your place soon." She said, grabbing her purse and heading to the elevator.

"Yes I'll see you soon."

Gemma replied as she left as well, headed for home.

Then back at her apartment, she dimmed the lights, lit candles opened a bottle of wine and then slipped out of her clothes. Now in nothing but her black lace bra and panties. Then she sat back, sipping a glass of wine waiting anxiously for Jessie to arrive.

It wasn't long and there was a knock at the door, unsure if it was Jessie or Keith she answered.

It was Jessie.

"Ah there you are, come on in. I opened a bottle of wine if you'd like some."

She said walking back to the sofa.

Jessie, stood still. Staring at Gemma.

"Sure I'll have a glass, but damn girl, look at you!"

She said smiling and walking over to join her.

Gemma poured her a glass of wine and handed it to her.

"Thanks, I thought I'd get comfortable for when you got here."

Gemma said.

While Jessie joined her on the sofa and leaned in then grabbing her face, she kissed her.

Gemma, shivered with her touch kissing her back, long and passionately.

"Why don't you, get comfortable too."

Gemma said.

Taking the wine glass from Jessie's hand and placing it on the coffee table.

Jessie, raised her eyebrows seductively.

"Mmhmm sounds good."

She said running her tongue across her lips then biting her bottom lip. Then standing up before Gemma, she started removing her clothes.

Gemma sat watching her, wanting her as she looked up at her, standing right there in front of her. She had on purple satin panties and purple lace bra, that her nipples showed right through.

Gemma reached forward and ran her long nails, up Jessie's inner thigh to her panties. Then reaching through the side, she caressed her smooth shaven pussy with her hand.

Jessie shivered and bit her bottom lip with a moan.

"Mmhmm you're getting me wet."

She said bending down and grabbing Gemma by the hair and kissing her again.

Then sliding off her panties, she straddled Gemma's lap, then unlatched and removed her bra and then Gemma's too.

Then as they sat there, topless. She pushed her breasts hard against Gemma's. Their nipples hard and sensitive as the rubbed against each other.

Gemma reached and latched on to Jessie's breast with her mouth and started to tease her with her tongue, while reaching back into her panties and sliding her fingers into Jessie's now very wet pussy.

The two of them, now very much ready for Keith to join them, there was a knock on the door.

"That will be Keith."

Jessie said, sliding off of Gemma's lap, and Gemma went to let him in.

"Hi ladies"

He said walking in.

"It looks like you two got started without me."

Gemma, smiled then leaned in whispering in his ear.

"Just getting ready for you, stud!"

Keith smacked her ass, then took off his shirt, tossing it on the floor.

"Mmhmm, well then. Let me join you ladies."

He said taking off his belt, unzipping his jeans and moving towards Jessie.

Jessie, reaching into his jeans. Took his cock into her hand and started stroking it. Gemma coming up behind him, slid his jeans right off, then started running her tongue and hands slowly down his body, all the way to his to firm and sexy ass. Then squeezing his ass with her hand, she then bent down and bit him.

His cock now rock hard in Jessie's hand, as she slide it into her mouth and started sucking him and teasing him with her tongue. Gemma now moving behind Jessie. Pressing her naked body hard against hers. She grabbed on to her breasts, squeezing them and twisting her nipples, while watching her as she rammed Keith's cock in and out of her mouth.

Keith getting hotter and hotter, started pushing himself forward hard. Forcing himself deeper into Jessie's throat. Gemma held Jessie's head, while Keith continued ramming his cock right into the back of Jessie's throat gagging her each time. While leaning forward and kissing Gemma, shoving his tongue into her mouth.

Then stopping, he pulled his cock out of Jessie's mouth.

"Turn over"

He said tapping her thigh.

Gemma pulled back and lay there, while Jessie turned over. Her face now in between Gemma's legs her pussy facing Keith.

Keith quickly rammed his cock deep into Jessie's now soaked pussy, while Jessie started kissing and licking Gemma's. She licked fast then slow, shoving her tongue inside of her then encircling her clit with her tongue. Then pushed her fingers inside of her and started fingering her hard.

Keith pushed hard and deep inside of Jessie's pussy. She moaned and screamed while continuing to eat Gemma's. The harder Keith rammed his cock, the harder Jessie rammed her fingers into Gemma, even moving to her ass, she fingered that too.

Gemma squirming and moaning with pleasure. Jessie screaming as she's pounded over and over and Keith's body shaking with pure erotic pleasure. The apartment echoing the sounds of pure sexual excitement.

The three of them going at each other,   each of them shaking and writing ready to cum. Jessie screaming as she's ready to cum all over Keith's cock, Gemma now hitting the heights of pure satisfaction starts screaming as her pussy cums and Jessie drives her tongue deep inside of her to eat her as she cums right into her mouth. Keith's body now shaking, but not ready to cum yet he pulls out and asks the girls to switch.

Gemma now on her knees and Jessie laying back in front of Gemma.

Keith now ramming his cock deep into Gemma and Gemma licking and fingering Jessie's already soaked pussy and licking her cum from deep inside of her, then sliding down she started fingering her ass. Jessie moaning and writhing about below Gemma.

Gemma panting and screaming while Keith's cock rammed her hard and fast, deeper with each thrust and just as she thought, he couldn't go any deeper, he rammed it even further. Her body totally out of her control, screaming so loud it's now hard to catch her breath. Her body starts to shake and she once again cums, soaking Keith's cock and her pussy drips as he pulls out. Then grabbing Jessie by the hips from below Gemma, he pulls her forward and rams his cock back into her and leaning down, he licks Gemma's soaked pussy while the cum drips from her. Then pulling out of Jessie, her moves to Gemma, pounding her again and then back to Jessie. Moving back and forth from each of them, pounding both girls over and over. Each of them moaning and screaming. Their naked bodies on top of each other both being pounding by Keith's hard cock. They both squirmed on top of each other, their hard nipples rubbing against each other. Kissing with tongues in each other's mouths. Both of them completely lost in the moment. Keith ramming them one at a time pushing so fast and so deep cries were forced from their throats.

His body shook with sheer pleasure, his legs feeling weak as the passion took over his body and he shivered with the feeling of his arising orgasm. He began to slow his thrusts, he groaned and then pulling out, he stroked his cock hard and fast, until his cum shot from him and all over both girls.

The three of them now there, completely satisfied and out of breath.

Gemma reaches for her wine.

"I sure need this right now, anybody else?"

Jessie grabs her glass and raises it to Gemma's.

" Me too, cheers girlfriend!"

Keith headed towards the kitchen.

" You girls enjoy your wine, I'm going to grab a beer."

Then they all, sat down together. Recovering from their evening of excitement and decided to watch a movie.

Sex Education

Looking over his text book, he watched her. Sitting with her legs crossed. Slit in her skirt, clear up to her thigh. Breasts just barely showing, through her sheer blouse. Hair pulled back in a bun, her glasses resting on top of her head.

He couldn't help but stare. Though forbidden, he wanted her. A senior in college about ready to graduate. He had watched her for years and always noticed her, watching him too.

He had heard the rumours, from so many others, that had been given the chance with her, a chance to be with her, in her own little after school detention.

She was his biology teacher, but in detention she taught a whole new form of biology and new lessons that he more then anything wanted to learn.

Though knowing it was wrong, he could never, build up enough nerve to take the chance. So day in and day out, he just watched her and at times noticed her watching back.

Then it happened, one day while watching her, she looked back and winked.

He was startled by it and not sure what to think, as she then started walking around the room.

Stopping as his desk, she put her hand on his shoulder. His heart started pounding in his chest and he could feel himself starting to sweat.

She bent down, her cleavage right there before him.

"Join me for detention after school."

She whispered in his ear.

He looked up at her, his voice cracking with nervousness as he replied.

"Yes, yes Ma'am,"

She winked and returned to her desk, where she watched him the rest of the afternoon.

Then as the bell rang and the other students quickly rushed out of the room, he stayed behind.

She got up from her desk and walked over to him.

"Meet me at the supply room in ten minutes"

She said, putting her hand on his shoulder she giving it a squeeze.

Then with a wink she left the room.

He quickly jumped up and nervously headed to the supply room, where he waited outside for her to arrive.

When she arrived, she quickly unlocked the door, then looked to make sure nobody else was around.

"Come on in here."

She said, directing him inside, then locking the door behind them.

There she stood in front of him, his heart pounding and his palms sweaty as he watched her.

She slowly unbuttoned her blouse, revealing her white lace bra that her nipples clearly showed through.

"I've seen you watching me, always looking over your textbook, staring with lust in your eyes. Do you like what you see now?"

She said opening her blouse further.

His voice cracked as he nervously answered.

" Yes Ma'am, yes I definitely do."

A bulge in his pants now becoming very noticeable as she walked towards him.

Then slipping her hand down his pants, she stroked him getting him even

harder. Then grabbing his hands, she put them on her breasts.

"Do you like?"

She asked, squeezing his hands holding her breasts.

"Show me, show me you like them"

She said slipping her blouse off and unlatching her bra allowing it to fall to the

floor.

Her breasts now bare in his hands, his body shaking nervously. He squeezed

them and even leaned in, to kissed them and tease her nipples with his

tongue.

His cock, now so hard in his pants, it ached. She unzipped his pants

and slid them off. Then taking him into her hand, she started stroking it fast.

She could tell he was nervous, as she got down on her knees in front of him.

"Let me relax you."

She said, pushing him into her mouth. His body immediately shook with the

feeling of his cock in her mouth as she sucked him faster and faster. All of him

in her mouth. His body becoming like jello, his legs shaking. He could barely

contain himself. He knew he was going to cum, but afraid to cum too soon he

tried to hold back. But the feeling of her mouth wrapped so tightly around him,

sent shivers through his body and it happened. His cum began to spurt and

shot right down her throat.

She moaned as swallowed every drop, then stood up before him and slid off

over skirt and panties.

"Do you want my pussy?"

She asked, pushing his head towards her.

"Taste it, taste my pussy."

She said, as she forced his face against her.

He started licking her, and pushing his tongue inside of her. Then shoving his fingers inside of her, he starting fingering her.

She moaned, as his fingers stroked in and out of her. His cock now once again hard, wanting her. Wanting to feel himself deep inside of her. He licked faster and faster, teasing her clit with his tongue. Her pussy now soaked and his fingers dripping wet inside on her, as he blurted out.

"I want you! I want to pound your pussy hard."

She moaned, as she bent over the counter.

"Well take it then."

She said, bending further down.

He came up behind her, he pushed his hard cock into her now soaked pussy. He pushed himself all the way in and started stroking in and out faster and faster. Her pussy wrapped tight around him causing his body to quiver. She moaned as he pushed as deep as he could possibly go, then started thrusting faster and harder. She started moving her hips in a circular motion, enticing him further as he continued to ram his cock inside of her. Then pulling away from him, she turned around and pushed him down into a chair. Then straddling him, she shoved him deep inside of her and started riding him, she twisted her hips and moved up and down. Fast then slow then fast again, her breasts in his face as he pushed his face between them and then grabbed on to her nipples and started pinching and twisting them.

She moaned as she rode him fast, driving him hard into her pussy. He groaned below her, his body overcome with pleasure.

She continued to move her hips in a circular motion circling his cock deep inside of her. Pushing him in and out, her body now shaking and ready to cum all over him. She moved faster and faster, now shaking uncontrollably she screamed and started panting, her body overcome with pleasure as she cummed all over for cock.

Feeling her cumming, aroused him to point he was ready to blow his load deep in her pussy, he started groaning loudly. Knowing his was about to come, she stopped him. Then rammed his cock into her ass. She pushed him harder and harder until he was all the way inside. She screamed as she pushed him inside and he groaned with even more pleasure as he could no longer contain it and his cum shot deep inside of her filling her ass.

She moaned as she pulled off of him, then leaned in and kissed his cheek.

"How's that for detention?"
She whispered in his ear.

Still lost in the moment, he leaned back in the chair, grinning from ear to ear and replied.

"I'll take that detention anytime."

She smiled and winked at him, handing him his pants.

"You better get dressed and head home. If you're here too long, people might get suspicious."

He got up and quickly got started getting dressed, while watching her, slip back into her skirt.

"You're so beautiful."
He said, starting at her.

She smiled, now buttoning her blouse back up.

"Thank you. Now come on, let's get going."

She said, opening up the door and shuffling him out.

Then putting her hand on his shoulder, she said.

" I can see you again next week and every Tuesday after that, are you in?"

He smiled and anxiously responded.

"Yes! Definitely I will see you then."

She winked at him, then turning to walk away she whispered.

"Perfect, until next time then."

Lawyered up

Sitting behind his desk, going over file after file, taking call after call. It had been a long week. In and out of the court room and mountains of paper work. He was a lawyer and partner in his firm.

He had a girlfriend, yet it was hard to find enough time to enjoy her or even have a social life. He was all work and no play a strictly business kind of guy.

His girlfriend a beautiful young woman with a business of her own, running a lingerie shop in the town square. Each of them so busy with work, that finding time to be together was difficult. They wanted it all though, career, relationship and even one day family, so took every opportunity they could, to squeeze in time alone together. It was never easy, some days it was a quick lunch break, other times in between meetings or his court dates. Then every once in a while, they managed to squeeze in weekends or even surprise visits.

They had done this for years and some how always managed to make it work, despite their friends and families doubts.

Suddenly there was a knock on his door. Confused, that his receptionist hadn't announced anyone. He called out.

"Hello? Come in."

The door opened and she walked. It was his girlfriend. She had on a long black coat and high heels. He was confused by this as it was the middle of summer.

"Hi love, this is a surprise. Is it raining out or something?"

He asked walking over and giving her a kiss.

She smiled, kissing him back. Then walking over to the door, she locked it. Turned around and dropped her coat.

There she stood before him, in nothing but black lace panties and black leather corset and black stiletto heels.

"I thought you could use a small break."

She said, walking slowly towards him, as he stood there almost speechless.

"I'm up for a break like this, any time."

He said, grabbing her arm and pulling her to him.

She kissed him, putting her tongue his mouth, while running her nails across the back of his neck.

He grabbed her breasts and squeezed them, then bending down, he kissed her neck then moved down to lick her cleavage.

His cock now getting hard in his pants, he tore off his shirt, then swiped the top of his desk clean and lay her back on it.

Then sliding off her panties, he put her legs up on his shoulders and slipped in between her legs, with his face right in her pussy.

Then spreading her apart, he started licking her and teasing her. Pushing his tongue inside of her to taste her, then pulling it out he pushed his fingers deep inside while continuing to lick her clit and tease her now soaked pussy.

He pushed his fingers hard and deep, first just a finger, then two then three. Pushing harder and faster even knuckling her at one point, while continuing to lick her faster and faster. She writhed about on his desk, moaning as her body filled with erotic pleasure.

"Oh yes, that's it, eat my pussy, eat it good."

She called out as she became lost in the moment and she lost all control of her senses with her arising orgasm.

Knowing she was ready go cum.He pulled his fingers out and rammed his tongue deep inside of her. Pushing it in and out as she squirmed moaning louder and louder. Her legs now shaking on his shoulders as erotic pulsations shot through her body and she started to cum. He licked her faster and drove his tongue deeper inside to eat the cum right out of her dripping wet pussy.

Then sitting up, she pushed him back into his chair. Then grabbing her coat, she reached into the pocket and pulled out handcuffs.

Then swinging them around on finger and looking at him with a devilish grin and biting her bottom lip. She straddled his lap and asked.

"Are you ready for this?"

He moaned, looking into her sexy green eyes and answered with a throaty growl.

"I sure am, give it to me!"

She grabbed his arms, then handcuffed his wrists to the chair. Then sliding down her black leather corset, she pushed her now naked breasts in his face.

He moaned pushing his face in between them licking her cleavage, then biting them hard, he left his teeth marks behind.

Now grabbing on to her nipple with his teeth, he bit and then sucked on it and teased it with his tongue.

Her nipples now rock hard, as she reached down and pushed his hard cock deep inside of her. She pushed him all the way in, so deep it hurt as she started riding him. Stroking him in and out of her up and down, pulling almost all the way out, then driving it right back in, harder and harder each time. Her breasts bouncing in front of his face, he continued to grab on to them with his mouth. Teasing her as his hard cock throbbed deep inside of her warm soaked pussy.

She moved faster and faster, then slowed down, teasing him and making him beg for more. His body convulsing below her as she moved quickly up and down on his cock. Each time he was almost ready to cum, she would slow almost stopping, making him go wild with excitement below her.

"I don't want you to cum yet. "
She said, as she slowed right down.

"Not until you pound my ass."
She said, getting up off his lap.

He moaned.

"Mmhmm take these cuffs off then and bend over my desk. So Daddy can finish."

He demanded, as she removed the cuffs. Then turning around, she leaned over his desk, with her ass right there for the taking.

He came up behind, then spreading her ass apart, he started to push himself inside of her. The tip of his cock so aroused it was swollen, so it hurt going in. She screamed and jerked almost pulling away as he pushed harder and further. Her ass hurt but at the same time it turned her on. She moaned as she felt him moving deeper and deeper inside of her. Filling her ass tight with his cock as he started pounding her. He pushed it hard and fast, so deep inside of her she could barely stand it. Now hurting so bad, she almost wanted to pull away but she didn't. She grabbed on to the side of the desk, so hard her knuckles turned white. Screams now being forced from her throat with each thrust, her naked breasts smacking against his cold desk. Her body completely his. Being pounded over and over. He moved so fast she could no longer control the sounds coming from her mouth. She moaned, she screamed, she groaned and when he slowed she panted trying to gain control. But her body was out of her control and his now so aroused he groaned loudly as he jerked ramming himself harder inside of her and his body started to shake. She was hurting and ready to stop him, but feeling his body, jerk. She knew he was ready to cum so hung on as she cried out.

"Cum for me, fill my ass with your cum Daddy."

Hearing her crying out, sent him wild as he quickly pushed harder and faster.

Then as he started to cum, his body jerked and convulsed and he groaned loudly with pleasure as his cum shot from his cock filling her ass to the brim. Then with a few more small thrusts, he pulled out. Soaked with cum and her ass dripped from him.

"Now that's what I call, a good break!"

He said, slapping her thigh as she sat up.

"Happy you enjoyed it."

She replied kissing him on his lips.

Then pulling her corset back up and slipping back into her panties. She grabbed her coat.

"I'll let you get back to work now. See you Saturday?"

She asked.

Putting his clothes back on, he smiled and replied with a moan.

"Mhmm you sure will love."

Then winking and blowing him a kiss, she headed out.

Walking right past his receptionist, who by the look on her face. Had heard everything that had just happened.

"Have a nice day."

She said, stepping into the elevator."

How my son seduced me.

Last few miles on the drive. Headed home from school for the summer, Tim and his buddies had finished a week early.

Looking into the back seat.

"Hey bud, did you tell your mom you're coming home early?"

His friend asked.

"No I figured I'd surprise her, she'll probably already be sleeping by the time we get there though."

Tim answered.

His friend continued.

"I'd love to see that! Damn dude, your Mom is so hot! Nearly cream my pants just thinking about her."

Tim laughed as he replied.

"Wow man, taking it a little far aren't you?"

"I have to admit though she is hot. You should see her when she sleeps. All she ever wears is her bra and panties."

His friend slapped the steering wheel then yelled.

"Dude, no way! I'd be on her like white on rice."

"She makes me wish, I was adopted."

Then as they pulled onto Tim's street, his friend continued.

" I could always stay over at your place tonight."

Tim laughed.

"No not tonight, bad enough I'm showing up a week early without letting her know."

"Come by tomorrow though, we can hang out by the pool."

His friend was all for that.

"A chance to see your Mom in her bikini again, I'm there!"

"Okay, I'll give you a shout, tomorrow then."

He said as Tim got out of the car.

Then grabbing his bags, he waved.

"Okay great, thanks for the lift. Talk tomorrow then."

Then he headed inside.

"Mom, I'm home. Where are you?"

He yelled into the kitchen, with no response.

So headed up to his room. As he got to the top of the stairs, he could hear the shower running and looked down to hall, to see the bathroom door half way open. Unable to resist, he walked over to take a peek. All he could see, was his Mom's silhouette through the shower curtain, but it turned him on and he was getting hard in his pants. Though he never admitted the whole truth to his buddy, he was very attracted to his Mom.

He stood there watching her through the shower curtain. Fantasizing about being with her. Imagining being in there with her, washing her breasts, her pussy and grabbing that tight ass of hers.

The bulge in his pants, now so big he had to unzip and reaching in he stroked himself.

Knowing she would be getting out soon, he stepped away from the door and moved out of sight. Where he waited for the right moment, to catch her naked coming out of the shower.

As he stood there, with his cock hard in his pants, he heard the water turn off and the shower curtain open. Then he waited just long enough for her to step out and he walked over to the door.

There she was, standing completely naked and dripping wet, right in front of him.

He stood still, frozen on the spot and just stared.

Noticing him she jumped and grabbed her robe.

"Tim, oh my God you're home!"

"I never realized anyone was here, when did you get home?"

She asked, with a shocked look on her face.

He quickly answered as he tried to turn away, so she couldn't see the very noticeable bulge protruding from his pants.

"I just got here a few minutes ago, I thought I'd surprise you."

She laughed.

"Well that you definitely did, my boy!"

She said as she looked and noticed, him trying to hide his obvious Hard on.

"Hmm I see, you liked what you saw."

"It's okay Tim, you don't have to hide it. I'm actually kind of flattered by it."

She said, as she shuffled by headed to her room.

Tim, now so turned on by it all, went to his room. His cock was so hard in his pants, he needed to relieve himself. He dropped his pants and lay on his bed. Stroking himself while thinking about her naked and dripping wet. He stroked himself faster and faster, then just as he was about to cum. She walked in and startled him.

"Oh my Tim! I'm so sorry, umm I'm just making coffee. I thought maybe you would like to join me, but I see you're busy."

She said blushing and quickly turning around.

He jumped up, stopping her.

"Wait, don't go?"

He said grabbing her arm.

"Why don't you stay, you could give me a hand."

She was shocked and unsure how to respond.

"Give you a hand? What exactly do you mean by that?"

She asked.

Tim leaned in, kissed her neck and whispered.

"I think you know the answer to that."

"Come on Mom, you're on your own all the time. You must get lonely."

"We would be doing each other a favour."

Still surprised by what she was hearing, she pulled back as she answered.

"Tim, it wouldn't be right."

He grabbed her, kissing her again as he reached into her robe and grabbed her breast, giving it a squeeze.

Then whispered in her ear.

"Come on, you know you want to."

She moaned feeling his hands on her breasts.

"I don't know Tim."

She said trying to walk away, but she couldn't. His touch drew her in, she had been alone for so long, the temptation was too strong.

She turned back, grabbed him and kissed him as she cupped his balls with her hand.

Tim groaned untying her robe and slipping it off of her. Then grabbed her pussy and started pushing his fingers inside of her and bending down he bit on to her nipple.

Her legs started to feel like jelly, shaky. As she stood there with him fingering her faster and faster and she was stroking his hard cock with her hand.

"Get on the bed."

He whispered into her ear.

"I want to eat your pussy and you can suck my cock."

He said, leading her to his bed. Then laying her down, he climbed over her, with his cock dangling right above her mouth.

Then bending down, he buried his face in her pussy and started licking her. He licked her fast and shoved his tongue deep inside of her, teasing her as she started to squirm below him and she reached up pushing his cock into her mouth and started pushing him deep into her throat, stroking him in and out of her mouth, faster and faster. He continued licking her now soaked pussy, as he started driving his fingers in and out of her and even fingered her ass. She moaned and squirmed about, her breathing got faster as the pleasure took over her body. Him now so lost in the moment, started thrusting, taking over and ramming his cock deep into her throat. Hitting the back of her throat and gagging her with each thrust.

Hearing the gagging sounds coming from her throat, made him hotter as he started licking her pussy faster and faster, then driving his tongue inside to taste her while he pushed his fingers into her tight ass. She writhed about below him, ready to cum as she screamed out.

"Yes, yes! Oh my God yes!"

He licked faster and encircled her clit with his finger tips. Her body started to convulse and her legs shook, she cried out with pleasure at this point, unable to even catch her breath. As she started to cum, soaking his face. Him ready to cum himself as he pulled away and rolled over.

"On your knees."

He demanded, smacking her thigh.

She quickly rolled over and got up on her knees.

He came up behind her and drove his rock hard cock, deep into her soaked pussy. He pushed it long and hard, in and out. His body jerked with each thrust. As he moved faster and faster, smacking her ass then pulling her hard against him to pound her even harder. She moaned and screamed, as his pounding thrusts forced the sounds to shoot from her throat. Him now pounding her so hard, it was impossible to tell where his thrusts began and ended. His body shaking, he groaned loudly with his impending orgasm. As he quickly pulled out, then rolling her over he shoved his cock between her breasts he pressed them hard against it as he started sliding it up and down towards her face. Faster and faster, until finally his body began shaking and his cum started to shoot from his cock, he pushed up quickly and it shot all over her mouth and face. She licked her lips, then wiped the rest with her hand then licked it clean.

Watching her eat his cum, was turning him on again and he wanted more. He wanted her ass. So he pushed his cock towards her.

"Get me hard again, I want your ass now."

He demanded.

She moaned taking his cock into her hand as she started stroking it.

Then leaning in, she pushed him back into her mouth and started sucking him again. Slow then fast, then stopping to tease the tip with her tongue, then rubbing his balls and running her nails up and down his inner thigh. Then stroking him faster and faster in and out of her mouth. His cock now hard again as she stopped at the tip, popping off to tease him further.

His body now overcome and ready for more, he pulled out.

"Roll over."

He demanded tapping her thigh.

She rolled over and he quickly came up behind her. Then spreading her ass, he spit on her and started pushing his cock into her ass. He pushed little by little. She pulled forward and he pulled her back. Then slapping her ass he pushed harder forcing himself deeper.

She cried out as it hurt, hearing her cries made him push harder, finally ramming himself all the way into her ass. She let out a loud scream, he bent forward and bit her ass hard, she jumped and moaned as he then started to pound her harder and harder. Her ass wrapped tight around his cock. So hard that his body was aroused to the point he was once again ready to cum.

Him groaning loudly, cries of pain shooting from her throat simultaneously. As his thrusts started to slow and his body shivered. His body now completely taken over, her ass hugging his cock so warm and so tight made him shake and his cum began to shoot from him in spurts and filling her ass full of his hot cum.

Then pulling out, he flopped down on the bed beside her. Her ass soaked and dripping from his cum.

"That was amazing."

He blurted out.

Her still in shock, at what had gone on, replied.

"Umm yes it was, but I'm not sure how to feel about this. You're my son!"

He rolled over and kissed her cheek and whispered.

"Yes your son and more now. Let's just enjoy it."

Then as he sat up to get dressed, he added.

"Definitely makes my home comings more interesting."

"Now how about that coffee? Still want some?"

She got up and slipped her robe back on.

"Sure, I'll go make some. I'll see you downstairs."

She said with a wink, then headed down.

Night shift nurse

Pulling back the curtain, she walked in and turned on the light.

"It's time for your sponge bath, Jill."

She said as she helped her up.

She was Candy, the night shift nurse and all the young men on the floor, were all in to her. Flirting with her every chance they got, some even trying to get further with her and rumour has it, some did.

He sat in the bed next to Jill, just a curtain separating them. Every night, he watched while sexy nurse Candy came in and gave Jill her sponge bath. With the lights on and the two of them in just the right position, he could see their every move and the perfect silhouette of Jill's naked body being washed by the nurse Candy.

Watching them was always a turn on and he fantasized about doing Candy, right there in his hospital bed.

He watched, as she washed Jills breasts, her hands moving all over them and then down her sides and her back. Washing every inch of her, while Jill moaned , saying how good it felt.

"How does that feel?"

Nurse Candy asked.

"Absolutely amazing."

Jill answered with a moan.

He sat watching, his hand down his pants as he now, had a very obvious hard on.

He wanted Candy so bad, he'd been watching her every night and played with himself every time he saw her.

There was nothing to prevent him from having sex and he was determined to find a way to seduce her and have his way with her.

Candy finished up with Jill and was headed out, he called to her.

"Nurse, nurse Candy?"

She turned and came back and over to see him.

"Yes Jaxon, did you need something?"

She asked.

"I've got a bad cramp in my neck, could you fix my pillows?"

He asked with a flirty grin.

Leaning over, she plumped up his pillows and then started to rub his neck.

"Does that feel better? Where exactly does it hurt?"

She asked.

The way she was leaning over him, he could see right down into her cleavage.

"Right there, yea that's it. That feels so much better."

He said, enjoying every second of her hands on him.

His cock now rock hard and impossible to hide as it stuck up below the sheets.

Candy continued rubbing his neck but couldn't help but notice.

"Well now"

She said

"I see, it must me feeling a lot better."

"You seem to really be enjoying this."

"Yes, I definitely love to have your hands on me."

He said, winking at her.

Then he moved to her ear and whispered.

"That's all for you, I want you bad."

Candy stopped rubbing his neck then leaned in and whispered back to him.

"I like what I see."

Shocked he moaned, then reached and grabbed her breast. She stopped him.

" No not here"

She whispered.

"I'll come get you in a bit."

"You just stay ready."'

She said, as she winked and left his room.

Jaxon wasn't sure, if she was serious, or just playing with him. As he sat there, envisioning everything he wanted to do to her.

As he stared off, lost in his own thoughts. He heard Candy come back in. She was pushing a wheel chair.

"Jump in Jaxon, I have to bring you down for some tests." She said with a seductive wink.

He jumped right up and got into the wheel chair with no questions asked. Anxious to see where she would take him.

Candy wheeled him down the hall and right into the nurses lounge, where she locked the door behind them.

"We can't be long."

She said, as she stood before him. Unbuttoning her top. Her white lace bra

now showing and her large firm breasts popping out the top.

Jaxon's cock immediately got hard as he watched her moving

towards him. Then leaning down, her breasts now almost falling into his face.

She asked.

"Do you like what you see?"

Jaxon moaned as he replied.

"Definitely, I definitely do."

As he reached and grabbed her breasts, then pulling her to him. He licked

her cleavage, then pulling her breasts completely out of her bra. He kissed

and nibbled at her now rock hard nipples.

Candy got down on her knees, between his legs. Then

reaching into his pants, she took his cock into her hand and started stroking it

and reaching down she caressed his balls. His cock rock hard and ready for

action. As she then pulled it out and leaning down, she pushed it into her

mouth.

She stroked him in and out of her mouth, taking him deeper

and deeper each time. While continuing to rub his balls with her hand and

then stroking his cock as she pulled up with her mouth. Then stopping to pop

off at the tip, she encircled it with her tongue. His body was shivering with

pleasure, the excitement taking over, as he pushed the back of her head.

Pushing himself deeper into her throat and gagging her. She moved faster

and faster his cock now so hard and swollen. Ready to explode. He filled her

mouth, her lips now wrapped so tight around him. He could barely stand it

anymore. His body began to shake and he moaned uncontrollably, as his

cum shot right down her throat and she swallowed every drop. Then pulling off, she licked the final little drips off the tip and started running her tongue. Up and down him and moving to his balls, she pushed them into her mouth and sucked and licked them. Trying to get him hard once again.

Jaxon moaned with sheer pleasure, as he watched her. Then reaching up her skirt, he moved his hand towards her pussy. Only to discover, that she was wearing crotchless lace panties and her pussy was wet and ready for him.

"Mmhmm you're so wet."
He moaned, as he started pushing his fingers deep inside of her.

Candy spread her legs further for him, moving closer so he could play with her. Then pushing her pussy towards his face and forcing his head down.

"Lick my pussy, make me cum"
She demanded.

Jaxon leaned forward and pushed his face into her pussy and began licking it ferociously, shoving his tongue deep inside to taste her then licking her clit he encircled it with his tongue and even bit her, forcing a shriek to shoot from her throat.

He licked faster and faster, her legs shaking as her arising orgasm made it almost impossible to stand still. She moaned and shivered, feeling his tongue pushing deep inside of her and licking the whole inside of her pussy. Sounds of pleasure now uncontrollably coming from her throat. As she quivered and her pussy began to cum all over Jaxon's face.

Jaxon moaned as he licked her cum right out of her, while squeezing her ass so hard that his nails dug in.

His cock now so hard again, it ached. As Candy then turned around, with her back to him and moving down. She pushed his cock into her soaked pussy. She pushed him deeper and deeper, until he could go no further. Now all the way inside of her. She started moving her body up and down. Slow, the fast, then slow again. Teasing him with each thrust into her pussy. Wrapped so tightly around his cock, the warm wet feeling as she stroked up and down, drove him wild. He grabbed her ass then moved up, reached around to grabbed her breasts as she moved faster and faster on his lap. His cock

Pounding in and out of her and throbbing deep inside. She moved so fast, up and down pushing him so deep he could feel the back of her pussy pound hard against the tip of his cock. His body now ready to burst, his cock tingling with pleasure inside of her, as he began to shake and moan. Then with sudden jerks of his body, the sensation took over and he shot his hot cum deep inside of nurse Candy.

She moaned, feeling his hot cum filling her up and she twisted her hips teasing him further, until he was completely satisfied.

"How was that, for medical care?"
She said getting up off his lap.

Still over come with the sheer pleasure. Jaxon slipped his cock back into his pants.

"Without a doubt, the best medical care I've ever gotten."
He replied.

Candy, buttoned her top back up and fixed her skirt.

"Happy to help."

She whispered with a wink and a kiss to his cheek."

Then she wheeled him back to his room and he got back into his hospital bed,

"I'm sure, you could use the rest now."

She said, adjusting his bed for him.

" Yes thank you nurse Candy."

He said with a huge smile and a wink.

She winked back headed out of the room.

"Perfect, sweet dreams then."

She said.

Yes Sir

Standing in the kitchen, cooking dinner. Wearing nothing but a sheer white dress, that you could see right through. She waited for him to come home.

Her husband, her love and her master. Their relationship, wasn't one that many of their friends and relatives understood, but for them, It was perfect.

Taking care of him was what she lived for. What ever he wanted, she gave him. They did have their boundaries and all things were open for discussion, but for the most part. It was unneeded and boundaries were rarely crossed.

She was his, mind body and soul and it was how she wanted it. Pleasing him, was always her number one priority.

She knew his likes, his dislikes and he knew hers.

He worked hard at his job, to care for her and give her all she that needed and in return. She took care of him in every way possible. She took care of their home, made sure he had good meals, he was well cared for and she fulfilled all of his sexual fantasies. What ever he wanted he got.

She heard the front door open, she knew he was home, as always her heart started pounding. She loved him
So deeply and so passionately, that her heart raced when ever she saw him.

Walking into the kitchen, he saw her standing by the counter. In that sheer dress, he so loved. She was just as he wanted her and the very sight turned him on.

He walked up behind her, grabbed her ass and bit her neck.

"Hello beautiful, Daddy's home."
He whispered into her ear.

She smiled, turning to him and she kissed him on his lips.

"Welcome home, how was your day!"

She asked.

He pulled her to him, then grabbing her breasts with his hands and squeezing them hard, he answered.

"Not too bad, could have been better I suppose."

"Now, why don't you welcome Daddy home properly."

He said smacking her ass.

She nodded.

"Yes Sir"

She said getting down on her knees and unzipping his pants.

Then taking his cock into her hand, she started to stroke him up and down, while leaning in to lick the tip, getting him hard. Then she pushed him deep into her mouth and started sucking him. Pushing him in and out of her mouth, slow then fast. She gripped on with her hand and stroked it hard while continuing to push him in and out of her mouth. She reached in a cupped his balls in her hand. She rubbed them and teased them. His cock now so hard, it filled her mouth as she moved faster and faster. Him now so aroused. He grabbed her head and held it as he started to push himself, ramming himself deep into the back of her throat. She gagged with each thrust, her eyes watering and tears running down her face.

He pushed faster and faster, harder each time.

"Take it, suck my cock, suck it good."

He demanded as he continued forcing himself in and out of her mouth.

She moaned in between gagging, as his cock rammed in and out of her mouth. His thrusts started to slow, his legs shaking as she took over, pushing him in and out of her mouth, then pulling him out and sliding her tongue up and down to tease him, then sucking some more and popping off at the tip and encircling it with her tongue. His body now out of his control, he shakes and jerks as his cock moves slowly in and out of her mouth and his hot cum begins to shoot out and right down her throat and she swallows.

Then pulling him out of her mouth, she licks the tip making sure to get every drop.

"That's my girl."

He says putting his hand on her head.

"Now finish up cooking dinner and afterwards, you can give Daddy a little desert."

He said as she got up and he smacked her ass.

She moaned and kissed him.

"Sounds perfect"

She said with a wink, as she went back to cooking.

Not long after it was time to eat. She served him his dinner and they sat down at the table across from each other. They talked about each other's days and even cracked jokes with each other.

They were just like any other married couple in that way. It was just their different ways with their sexual relationship and her submissive behaviours that through other people in their lives off. Many never agreed with their life style, but for them they were happy and content in their lives and enjoyed every minute of each other.

As they sat eating their meal and chatting, she slid her toes up his leg from under the table. He reached across and squeezed her thigh in a seductive manor. Then grabbed her pussy, giving it a squeeze.

"This is mine, is that clear?"

He said with a growl.

She smiled blowing him a kiss.

"Yes Daddy."

They finished up their meal and she started to clear the table. He reached over and smacked her ass. Then lifted her gown and growled.

"Take it off."

He demanded, watching her as the light shining through her gown revealed her naked body underneath.

She smiled as she slowly unbuttoned and allowed her gown to fall to the floor. Then continued to clear the dishes.

He watched her, naked in the kitchen cleaning up from dinner. The glow of the overhead lights reflecting off her breasts as she scrubbed the pans.

Becoming aroused, he reached into his pants and stroked his cock, getting himself hard. He was ready, he wanted her.

Walking up behind her, he reached over her and turned off the running water. Then gently kissed her neck and then continuing down her body. He ran his tongue, all the way down to her ass. Then biting her ass, hard enough to leave a mark, he asked.

"Do you want me?"

She looked passionately into his eyes as he continued.

"Tell me!"

"Get down on your knees and beg for me."

He said pushing his hard cock up against her.

She dropped to her knees and looked innocently up to him.

"I want you, please sir, I want you now."

He growled pulling her up and bending her over the counter.

" That's my girl."

He said, as he bent her further over and started pushing his fingers deep into her pussy, in and out, while biting and kissing her neck and back.

She moaned, her pussy now soaked and wanting him inside of her.

"I want you Sir, I want you now!"

Hearing her words aroused him further as he pushed his rock hard cock into her soaked pussy. He never took it slow, as soon as the tip was in, he rammed it inside of her. So hard that the tip hit the back of her pussy, forcing a cry of pain to shoot from her throat.

He rammed it fast and hard, she screamed with pain but never stopped him.

"Who's a good girl?"

He asked as he continued to ram her pussy harder and harder, so deep that it was hard to tell, where each stroke ended and the next began.

She cried out in response to him.

"I'm a good girl, I'm a good girl!"

Her body bent over the counter, her breasts slapping against the cold marble countertop as his cock pounding in and out of her now dripping pussy.

Her screams now so loud, he reached around covering her mouth with his hand, muffling the sounds.

"That's a good girl."

He said smacking her ass hard as he continued.

"Cum for me, come on cum for Daddy."

Her body so overcome, his words echoing through her head. As she began to shake, her pussy beginning to pulse, as his thrusts slowed. Then reaching his hand between her legs, he encircled her clit with his fingertips. Her legs became like jelly and waves of pleasure took over her body. She bit her lip, trying to hold back the screams of pure erotic pleasure about to shoot from her throat. As she began to cum and her entire body was at his mercy.

He grabbed her by the hair pulling her head back as he whispered in her ear.

" Time for me to finish, are you ready?"

Knowing what was coming, she braced herself.

"Yes Sir."

With that, he slid his fingers into her pussy, soaking them with her cum and wiped them on her ass.

Then moving his cock to her ass, he started to push himself inside. He pushed and pushed getting just the tip inside.

"Are you ready? I'm going all in."

She gripped onto to the edge of the counter.

"Yes Sir, I'm ready."

Then with one hard fast thrust, he pushed himself all the way into her ass. He scream shot from her throat and tears streamed from her eyes. It hurt, it burned but she never stopped him .

His hand by her face as she took his finger into her mouth. The sensation of her sucking his fingers, always aroused him to the point of orgasm. He pounded her ass over and over tears still running down her face while she sucked his finger teasing him. He begins to groan, his body jerks with pleasure as his arising orgasm takes over. He pounds her harder and faster pushing so deep he can't go any further. He shakes as sounds of pleasure shoot through the room, then his thrusts slow as he begins to cum deep in her ass. Now completely overcome by pleasure, he slowly starts to pull out. His body jerks a few more times as the last drops shoot from him.

Then pulling out, he slaps her ass as he watches his cum slowly drip from her.

"Better clean yourself up, before finishing the kitchen."

He whispered as he kissed her forehead with a smile

Big Tipper

"Hello, I'm Kim, Can I get you something to drink?"

She said, setting a menu down on the table.

He looked up at her with a flirty grin.

"Sure, I'll take a rye and ginger love."

He said with a wink.

She blushed taking his order. He was a young good looking guy, perfect hair,dimples on his cheeks and clearly built. His eyes were ocean blue and they glistened when he looked at her, giving her chills.

She walked over the the bar to grab his drink and couldn't help but look back at him.

"Wow, did you see that guy at table two?"

She said to the bar tender, who looked over and bit her lip when she saw him.

" Mmhmm look at him?"

She said staring at him, then making his drink.

"Lucky you, getting to serve him tonight?"

She said handing Kim his drink.

"Oh I know! He's definitely easy on the eyes and oh my that body!"

She said, turning to head back to his table.

The bar tender laughed as she yelled out jokingly.

"Go get him girl!"

She looked back blushing, then handed him his drink.

"Have you decided what you'd like?"

She asked, so drawn in by him, her heart was pounding.

Noticing her blushing, he winked and gave her his order, then added.

"And does that come, with you on the side, beautiful?"

Kim's cheeks now beet red and she giggled looking at his gorgeous smile.

"Thank you. Is there anything else?"

She asked.

He winked and looked into her eyes.

"Sure. You can tell me what time you get off tonight?"

Unsure what to say, or if he was even serious. She giggled as she walked away to hand in his order.

Back at the bar, the bar tender was still staring his direction.

"Damn girl, I'd be on him like bees to honey"

She said nudging Kim standing at the order window.

"Does he talk, as sexy as he looks?"

She asked.

Kim still blushing at the very thought of him, answered.

"Oh my God yes!"

"He even asked me what time I get off tonight."

The bar tender smacked her hand on the bar.

"Did you tell him?" She asked.

"Damn girl, go for it!"

She laughed as she headed back to his table with his order.

He looked up at her.

"Is that smile for me?" He asked.

"I sure hope so, I'm Jaxon by the way."

She blushed.

"Is there anything else I can get you?" She asked.

"A drink refill maybe?"

Jaxon smiled handing her his glass.

"Sure I'll have one more. If you're shift is done soon, I'd love for you to join me."
He said with a wink.

Still unsure what to think, but throwing caution to the wind, thinking "hey you only live once."

She replied.

"Sure, why not, I get off in an hour. If you want to hang around that long."

He winked as he answered.

"I definitely do. I'll finish my dinner and then wait for you at the bar."

She smiled, turning to go back to get his refill.

"Perfect, I'll be right back with your drink."

As she walked up to the bar, with a huge grin on her face. Making it obvious to the bar tender.

"Girl, that smile says it all."
She said.

Kim nodded.

"Yes I agreed to meet him here at the bar after my shift."

She said with a giddy giggle.

The rest of her shift seemed to drag. She was anxious to have drinks with Jaxon. She kept looking in his direction and noticed, every time, he was watching her too.

The last half hour of her shift, was busy.

She dropped Jaxon's bill off at his table.

"Thirty minutes left, figures it would get busy now."

She said

Jaxon winked as he replied.

"I'm sure it will pass quickly beautiful."

"Here's my card, be sure to give yourself a nice tip. Fifty dollars good?"

He asked.

She was shocked.

"Really? That is more then generous of you. Are you sure?"

She asked.

He winked as he answered.

"Yes I'm very sure."

Kim went over the bar, to pay for his order then returned his card to the table.

"I guess ill see you shortly at the bar." She said with a flirty smile.

He smiled back.

"You sure will doll."

Her shift, quickly ended. She clocked out and headed out to the bar, to meet Jaxon.

Seeing her headed towards him, he stood up. Then took her hand and helped her on to the stool.

"What would you like to drink my dear?"

He asked signalling to the bar tender, they were ready to order.

"Hmm. I'll take a cherry hooker, I guess."

She answered.

The bar tender took their order and winked a Kim, as if to say " way to go girl."

Jaxon and Kim, sat at the bar chatting getting to know each other. Time seemed to pass quickly. What felt like only moments, had actually been hours and the bar was ready to close.

"Wow, last call already!"

Jaxon said with a sigh.

"I'm really enjoying being with you." Then putting his hand on hers, he continued.

"I'm not ready for it to be over yet."

Kim smiled, looking into his eyes.

"I'm not either."

"The time has passed too quickly."

"I don't live far from here, do you want to come by?"

She asked.

Without hesitation, Jaxon answered.

"I'd love to."

Kim smiled, then wrote her address down on a napkin.

Jaxon took it as they got up to head out.

"Thanks, I'll likely just follow you though anyway."

With that, they headed off to her apartment. This wasn't something, Kim would normally do. However with Jaxon, there was a connection. Something more, then she had felt on other dates and she needed to see where things led.

They headed inside, she turned on the lights, nice and dim. Then lit a few candles and turned on some quiet music.

Jaxon made himself comfortable on the sofa.

"Nice place you have."

He said.

As she joined him.

"Thank you, it's perfect when It's just for me."

Jaxon put his arm around her and pulled her close. Then with her head nestled on his chest. They sat and talked while listening to music.

Kim had become, very comfortable with him. As she started running her nails up and down his leg and inner thigh.

Jaxon enticed, squirmed a little as he rubbed her back then leaned down. Taking her face in his hands. He kissed her sweetly on the lips.

Kim looked passionately into his eyes as she turned to him and climbed on to his lap. Then straddling him, she kissed his neck and nibbled his ear lobes.

Jaxon's cock becoming hard in his pants. She could feel it, as she moaned and reached down to stroke it. From the outside of his jeans.

He grabbed her ass cheeks and squeezed them hard, then while kissing her neck, he reached down and unzipped.

His rock hard cock, now protruding from his jeans.

Kim reached down and started to stroke him up and down and reaching inside she cupped his balls with her hand.

He moaned, as he started slowly unbuttoning her blouse.

She stopped him, then finished herself and removing her blouse, she tossed it across the room.

Then she slid off her bra. Her breasts, nipples now hard. Right there, ready for him.

He squeezed her breasts, then leaning forward. He teased her nipples with his tongue, encircling them, then lightly biting them with his teeth.

Her panties becoming wet, as his touch aroused her in a way that was intense.

Then sliding down on to the floor, on her knees, between his legs. She slid off his jeans then slowly ran her tongue up his inner thigh, right to his balls. Where she then started to lick them and tease him further, by running her tongue right up to the tip of his cock and then back down again.

Now extremely hard, ready to burst. He grabbed her head. Pulling her close, he pushed his cock into her mouth.

She moaned, as she started sucking him. Pushing him in and out of her mouth. His body jerked with pleasure. Her hand caressing his balls while she pushed his cock deep into her throat. Him now so aroused, he grabbed her head and pushed it forcing himself further. Ramming his cock so hard into the back of her throat. She gagged and her eyes started to water.

He continued ramming his cock in and out of her mouth. He was now completely in control, as she gagged over and over and tears streamed down her face.

His body began to convulse with pleasure, his cock now so hard in her mouth, she could barely handle it. He moaned, he shook. His thrust slowing, as his hot cum started to shoot from him and right down her throat.

She swallowed every drop, then ran her tongue up to lick to tip. He shuttered with the feeling of her tongue licking him dry.

As he reached down her pants and grabbed her ass then slid to the front to feel her now soaked pussy.

She stood up and slowly removed her pants. Now standing completely naked before him.

He moaned and pulled her close, then kissed her pussy and slid his fingers inside.

"I want this."

He said with a groan.

She smiled, moving closer.

"Then take it baby."

She said bending over in front of him.

Jaxon got up behind her, she leaned over the the back of the sofa. With one leg on and one leg on the floor.

He came up behind her and bent down to lick her pussy, tasting her and getting her even wetter. She moaned and squirmed, her pussy ached for him.

As he slowly pushed his cock inside of her, inching it bit by bit, teasing her making him want him even more.

She pushed her pussy hard against him forcing him all the way inside.

He groaned knowing how badly she wanted him. As he began pounding her pussy hard and deep.

With each deep thrust, she moaned loudly. Her breathing intensifying, as her body was overcome by pleasure.

He moved faster and faster, now so hard and deep, it hurt. She screamed with pain, but at the same time pleasure. Her body now his, as he continued to go at her hard and reaching around, he squeezed her breasts. The sounds of their bodies slapping together mixed with shrieks and moans of pure sexual satisfaction echoed through her apartment.

Her body now shaking, her breathing out of control as her pussy began to cum. Intense pulsations shooting through her, she screamed with pleasure. Hearing the sounds shooting from her throat. Aroused him further, as his body also began to shake and convulse and was brought to intense orgasm. He pulled his cock out and allowed his hot cum, to shoot across her ass. He moaned as he jerked releasing every drop. She moaned and panted below him. Both of them, exhausted yet completely satisfied.

Then getting up from the sofa, Jaxon pulled her up against him.

"Definitely a better night, then I had planned."

He said.

She smiled kissing his lips, then replied.

"Amazing night actually."

"Will I see you again?" She asked.

Jaxon kissed her on the forehead.

"You can count on it angel

Under the Mistletoe

In the silence, all that could be heard was the crackling of the fire and wind whistling

outside while the snow flew. The Christmas lights twinkling on the tree, while she hung

their stockings from the mantle.

He watched her, the light of fire and twinkling lights bouncing off her long blonde

hair.

Then as she bent down, to place gifts beneath their tree. He came up behind her and held mistletoe over her head.

Looking up, she smiled and stood up to kiss him.

He groaned as he grabbed her breasts with his hands and then kissed her neck.

She shivered with his touch, but pulled away.

" I need to get these stockings filled."

She said, raising her eyebrows and turning away.

He twirled her back around and pulled her up against him.

"How about you let me, fill your stocking first?"

He said leaning down to kiss her forehead.

She slapped her hand on his chest and gave him a seductive glare.

"You're insatiable."

She giggled while shaking her head.

He grabbed her ass hard, the slowly started to slide down her red silky pyjama pants.

"I don't deny that." He said.

"Now how about you give Daddy a Merry Christmas?"

She quivered as she reached into his pants and took his already hard cock into her hand.

"Mhmm somebody's ready."

She said getting down on her knees and sliding his pants down.

His cock rock hard, staring her in the face as she cupped his balls in her hand and began teasing him, while running her tongue down his inner thigh and back up to kiss and lick his warm balls.

His legs shaking, his body wanting more. He grabbed her head and pushed it to his cock. Then as she opened her mouth to take him inside, he rammed it, right down her throat. She gagged, her eyes watered as he started stroking himself in and out of her mouth.

He pushed himself hard and deep into her throat while holding her head against him. She gagged with each thrust. The sounds arousing him further.

Then suddenly, pulling out. He got down on his knees next to her.

"Lay down"

He demanded, and she lay down on the floor in front of the blazing fire.

Then straddling her, he pushed his cock back into her mouth, while he bent forward and began licking her already soaked pussy and pushing his tongue deep inside to taste her.

She moaned and squirmed below him, his cock moving in and out of her mouth while she stroked his balls and ran her nails down to a spot that drove him wild.

Her pussy dripping wet, her body quivering. As his tongue pushed deep inside of her and then pulling out he encircled her clit with the tip. The intense pleasure, taking over her body, as she moaned and her breathing intensified with her arising orgasm.

Knowing she was ready to cum, he moved faster in and out of her mouth, moaning with excitement. His body began to jerk, his legs shaking.

Then right as he was about I cum, he pulled out and allowed his hot cum to shoot across her breasts.

Feeling his cum shoot across her chest, made her squirm with pleasure and she shook as she herself was brought to orgasm.

Hearing the shrieks of pleasure shoot from her throat, made him lick faster and faster then burying his tongue deep inside of her to taste her hot cum. He continued to lick her, she squirmed with a pleasure so intense, she could barely take anymore. He ate her pussy for so long, he nearly licked her dry.

Their bodies sweaty and glistening from the twinkling lights, out of breath and so overcome by pleasure.

He now hard again, after eating her pussy for so long and hearing her cries of pleasure.

Tapped her on the ass.

"Roll over babe."

He instructed and she rolled over.

Then placing her legs up on his shoulders, he pulled her closer and pushed his cock deep into her pussy and began stroking in and out. Slow, then fast, then slow again. Then pulling nearly all the way out. He rammed in back in, so deep she let out a cry of pain.

He continued to pound her, hard and deep. Screams of both pleasure and pain involuntarily shot from her throat. She arched her back, as the erotic sensations took over her body.

Reaching down, she started encircling her clit with her finger tips.

Seeing this drove him wild. He moaned and bent forward taking her nipple into his mouth, teasing her with his tongue. Then biting her breast, forcing a shriek from her throat. He began to slow his thrusts. Pulling all the way out and then pushing slowly back in. Then moving his cock in a circular motion, her pussy wrapped tight around it. He could feel the pulsating deep inside of her begin. She moaned and cried out as she became lost in the moment. Her body now completely his. He started to move faster and faster, once again pushing so deep, he could go no further. She screamed as she began to cum, soaking his cock deep inside of her.

His body now beginning to shake, groans shooting from his throat. The sounds of pleasure filling the room as he began to slow his thrusts again and then with one last hard thrust deep inside. His hot cum shot inside of her.

Then as his pulled out, her pussy dripped from their cum that filled her to the brim.

Leaning down, he kissed her forehead.

"Now that's a Merry Christmas Eve!"

He whispered in her ear

Pool Boy

Standing at the window, she watched him. Tall, young and fit with an ass that called to her.

Shirtless in his tight little shorts, the muscles in his thighs and biceps bulging, while the hot sun glistened off his body.

He was her pool boy, young enough. She could be his mother, but the attraction to him was undeniably intense.

Three days a week, she watched him. Fantasizing about being with him and trying to find a way to make her fantasy a reality.

As she stood at the window, she reached into her top and fondled her own breasts. Then reaching into her pants. She started to finger herself and played with her clit. Her pussy soaked, as she dreamed of having him inside of her.

Feeling her watching him, he glanced up to the window. He knew that she always watched him. He had even noticed her playing with herself from time to time, as she stood watching. He purposely took his shirt off every time he arrived. Wanting to entice her, so he could see her getting hot for him.

He was attracted to her as well and imagined, taking her pool side and having his way with her.

Today was a super hot day, the sun was really beating down on him. He took a drink from his water bottle then poured it over his head, and let it run down his chest, knowing this would get to her.

As she watched the cool water run down his body, no idea he could see her. She encircled her clit with her fingertips. Her body tingling with pleasure, she was ready to cum.

Seeing her playing with herself, aroused him. He wanted her, but she was his boss. How could he approach her?

He continued to clean the pool, knowing she was watching him. He wanted to let her know he could see her, but when he got up the nerve to look directly at her, she was gone.

He finished up and left to load his truck and head home.

Thinking he was gone, she came outside in nothing but a towel, intending to swim naked.

Then just as she dropped her towel, there he was.

Forgetting his glasses, he had come back into the yard.

"Oh Ma'am!"

"I'm so sorry."

"I just needed to grab my sunglasses."

He said picking them up off the table, then turning to leave.

Getting up the nerve to make her move, she called out to him.

"Billy, wait!"

He stopped and turned back, looking down at the ground.

" Yes Ma'am?" He asked.

She picked up the sunscreen bottle and handed it to him.

"Could you help me get my back please?"

His voice cracked as he responded.

"Umm yea sure."

"I'd be happy too."

There she was, standing completely naked in front of him. He could feel a bulge growing in his shorts, his heart was pounding and sweat dripped from his brow.

He slowly rubbed sunscreen on her back, while looking at her beautiful ass in front of him. Wanting to just bend her over and take her right there.

She moaned as he rubbed her back.

"Mhmm that feels nice."

She said.

"Do you like what you see Billy?"

She asked, turning around to face him. Her breasts right there staring him in the face.

He looked into her eyes.

"Yes, yes I do Ma'am"

Then looking down, she could see his rock hard cock. Protruding from his shorts, she smiled and kissed his cheek.

"Yes I'd say you do."

"Is that for me darlin'"

"I sure hope so."

She asked, kissing him again, this time on the lips.

He moaned, pulling her closer to him.

"I've wanted you, for a long time"

He said, as he bent down and started licking and biting her nipples.

She ran her fingers through his hair, then pushed his head down to her pussy, already soaked and ready for a pounding.

He growled, as he started fingering her, while nibbling ferociously at her clit.

Her legs like jelly, she grabbed on to the table to keep her balance.

"That's right, eat my pussy!"

She said with a moan.

Her body now quivering, with waves of pleasure coursing through her.

Ready to cum, she pushed his head hard to her pussy. He pushed his tongue in and out, faster and faster, stopping only to suck on her clit. Bringing her to explosive orgasm. She screamed with pleasure, her legs shaking as her cum dripped from her and all over his face.

He was now so rock hard, he himself was ready to explode, as she got down on her knees in front of him.

Then pushing him into her mouth, she began sucking him. Slow then fast, then slow again. Taking all of him, deep into the back of her throat. While caressing and tickling his balls with her hand.

He moaned with pleasure, as her mouth slid up and down his cock, then popped off at the tip and she encircled it with her tongue. Teasing him and making him quiver and groan with pure satisfaction.

His cock now so hard, it pounded the back of her throat, gagging her as she sucked faster and faster. His body starting to jerk, his moans louder, heart pounding. As his cum started to shoot out. Then pulling him out of her mouth, she slid him in between her breasts allowing his cum to flow into her cleavage, while she slid him up and down.

He let out a loud moan of excitement, as he pulled away and bent down and latched onto her ass, hard with his teeth.

"Do you want it?

She asked.

Looking up with a yearning look in his eyes, he responded.

"Yes, yes Ma'am."

"I want to pound your beautiful, tight ass."

She smiled turning and pushing her ass towards him.

"Then take it Billy, take it."

She demanded.

His cock now hard once again, Billy got up behind her.

Then spitting onto her ass and wiping it in with his hand. He first started fingering her ass. Pushing his fingers deep inside of her, getting her ready for what came next. He pushed his fingers hard and deep. She squirmed and groaned. Wanting more, she cried out.

"Give it to me Billy!"

"Pound my ass."

Hearing her words aroused him in way that was almost animal like. As he moved his cock to her ass. Then not taking it slow or even gentle, he rammed it inside of her hard. She let out of shriek of pain, it hurt, it burned. She nearly stopped him, but instead she held on and let him keep going.

He moved quickly in and out of her ass, pushing harder and deeper each time. She screamed with pain the harder he went. He reached around and fondled her clit, mixing pleasure with the pain. Her pussy dripped, her ass hurt. His body shaking with pleasure, her ass so tightly wrapped around his cock.

He moaned as the pleasure took over, she involuntarily pulled away, he pulled her back ramming himself harder. She screamed, tears streaming from her eyes.

"Take it!"

"Take all if me!"

He yelled out, as his body started to convulse with his arising orgasm.

Hearing him so aroused, her pussy now starting to pulse, his cock filling her ass. Completely lost in the moment, she began to cum. She cried out with pleasure, begging him not to stop. He moved faster and faster, now taken over, by erotic sensations he'd never felt before.

He groaned a loud groan and started to jerk uncontrollably as his thrusts slowed and his cum shot deep into her ass.

Then stopping, with just a few more slight jerks. He started to slowly pull out. Her ass so filled his cum, she dripped as he pulled away.

She was completely lost in the moment, hard to believe, her fantasy had become reality.

As she looked into his sexy blue eyes and then kissed him on the cheek.

"Billy."

She said.

"You deserve a raise.

Dripping wet

Steam filled the bathroom, as the hot water rained down on her naked soapy body. The door left slightly open, music blasted as she sang along, dancing in the shower, as if nobody could hear her and if even if they could, she didn't care.

She was a single mom and the only other people around. Were her son and his best friend in the room down the hall.

She soaped up her body, playing with her breasts while she did. Caressing herself and encircling her nipples, now rock hard.

Down the hall, her son Matt sat playing video games with his friend Mitch. Neither of them, aware that just down the hall. His mother was showering and had forgotten to close the door.

"Is your Mom home?"

Mitch asked Matt.

"Ah yea, I think she's in her room."

"Why?"

 Matt asked.

Mitch glanced down the hall and could see steam coming from the bathroom.

"Oh I just wondered."

"I haven't seen her today."

" I actually need to use the washroom."

"I'll be right back."

Mitch said, getting up and heading out the door,

"Cool."

Matt replied continuing to play his game.

Mitch headed down the hall, knowing Matt's mother was in the shower. Hoping to catch a peek.

The closer he got, he could hear her singing and knew she wouldn't hear him approaching.

Walking up to the door, he could see her. Naked and dripping wet. The shower curtain was clear and hid nothing.

As he stood watching, he could see her playing with herself, pressed up against the shower wall. The hot water pouring down on her and the steam billowing up around her.

His pants becoming tight as his cock quickly hardened. He unzipped just slightly and reached in and touched himself.

He wanted so badly, to just tear off of his clothes and join her in the shower. She was his fantasy. All he could think about, was turning her around against the shower wall, bending her over and taking from behind.

In his mind, he'd already done it many times. Matt however, knew nothing about it. Mitch couldn't imagine, telling his best friend. That his mother was his biggest fantasy and he wanted to do her over and over again.

He leaned his head against the bathroom door and continued watching her. Her back now arched as she fingered herself and squeezed and caressed her breasts.

His hand in his pants, he stroked himself up and down. His body ached for her, he wanted to be inside of her.

Standing there, he was completely unaware, that she actually knew he was there.

She glanced over her shoulder, looking right at him and she winked.

He jumped, pulling his hand out of his pants. He zipped up quickly and went back down the hall to Matt's room.

"I'm back."

He said out of breath.

"I see that."

" Are you okay?"

" You sound winded."

Matt asked.

Sitting back down and picking up the game controller Mitch answered.

"Yea I'm great."

"No worries at all."

The boys sat, playing their game and all Mitch, could think about. Was the fact that Matt's Mom had caught him watching her.

Why didn't she say anything? Why wasn't she upset? Maybe she enjoyed it, he thought. Maybe she wants me, like I want her. Dozens of thoughts ran through his head.

"Hey, what's up?"

"Umm Mitch."

"You there?"

Matt said, nudging Mitch's shoulder.

Mitch jumped.

"Ah yea."

"Sorry, I got distracted there for a minute."

Mitch jumped back into the game, but right as they started to play again. Matt got a text from his girlfriend.

"Hey man."

"That's Marcy."

"She's done work and wants to see me for a bit."

"You can stay and keep playing if you want."

" I won't be all that long and my mom won't mind."

Matt said, as he grabbed his jacket.

"Oh, okay yea."

"I'll just wait around for you to get back."

"Go, have fun."

"Say Hi to Marcy for me."

Said Mitch, as Matt headed out.

Now sitting alone, Mitch wondered. If Matt's mom had finished in the shower. He pictured her, emerging from the shower, dripping wet. Then slowly drying off with her towel. Bending over to dry her feet and legs. Drying her perky breasts, her nipples hard from the cold air. His mind went to places that he only wished could happen. His cock was now once again, rock hard and the tip peeked out from the top of his pants.

He thought about going down the hall. To see what she was doing, but feared being caught watching her again.

He was completely lost in his own thoughts, staring off into space. When he felt a hand on his shoulder.

"Mitch."

She said.

It was Matt's Mom, standing right there beside him.

Not wanting her to see, his quite visible hard on. He grabbed a pillow and covered it up.

Then looking up to her, there she stood. Wearing nothing, but a short white satin robe.

"Yes Ma'am?"

He asked, with a shy look in his eyes.

" I saw you earlier."

"Why did you run away?"

She asked, as she sat down next to him.

Playing dumb, he responded.

"You saw me?"

"I'm sorry Ma'am."

"I shouldn't have been looking."

"I just couldn't help it, you're so beautiful."

Putting her hand on his thigh and looking into his eyes.

"Mitch, it's okay."

She said.

" every boy goes through a faze of curiosity."

He jumped and stopped her.

"boy? Every boy?"

"Ma'am, I'm not a boy anymore!"

"I turned 18 three months ago."

"I'm a man now!"

He said, grabbing her face and kissing her.

"See? A man!"

She pulled back, then raising her eyebrows and giving him a flirty smirk she replied.

" I see."

"So then, what does the man want?"

Totally stumped by her response, finding it hard to believe what was happening. He answered.

"Umm you."

"I want you Ma'am."

He muttered.

She pulled the pillow off of him, then unzipped his pants and slowly slid her hand inside.

"Mhmm, yes I would say you do."

"You've got me."

"Now, what are you going to do with me?"

He turned to her and slipped his hands into her robe and grabbed on to her breasts, giving them a squeeze. Then sliding her robe open, he leaned in and started to suck her nipples and even bit them gently.

She moaned, running her fingers through his hair. Then slipped out of her robe, allowing it to fall to the floor.

Then stood up, standing before him, completely naked. She grabbed his head and directed him towards her pussy.

He moaned as he buried his face into her pussy. Licking her clit and pushing his tongue deep inside of her. He encircled the inside of her pussy with his tongue and with his hand, he reached back and slipped his finger into her ass and started fingering it.

She squirmed, her legs shaking with pleasure coursing through her body. His tongue deep in her pussy, his finger pushing in and out of her ass.

Her pussy now dripping wet, soaking his face as she wriggled with the sensations of her arising orgasm. She moaned, she panted. Her body being overwhelmed with pleasure.

Knowing she was ready to cum, he moved to her clit, encircling it with the tip of his tongue. Then fingered her ass harder and faster.

She shrieked, her breathing intensified. Her body now shaking as she reached the heights if sexual satisfaction and her cum flowed from her, all over his face. He licked faster and faster, her pussy becoming overly sensitive.

She let out a scream.

"Yes, yes!"

"Oh Fuck yes!"

" Take me Mitch, take me!"

She demanded. Turning and bending over, her pussy right there and ready for him.

His cock, rock hard as he got up behind her and slid it deep into her soaked, dripping wet pussy.

"I'm going to pound you until you're dry!"

He shouted out, as he started to move. Thrusting his cock, in and out of her. Pushing himself so hard and deep she screamed with each thrust. He grabbed on to her hips and held her hard against him.

His body jerking with pleasure, pounding her harder and harder. Pulling almost all the way out and then ramming himself back inside. Her pussy so tight on his cock it almost hurt. She cried out with pleasure, her body all his.

"Pound me Mitch, pound me!"

She shouted.

Sensations intensified as he continued to go at her. Her pussy now starting to contract, as yet another orgasm began. She shrieked with excitement so taken by the pleasure, now almost hard to breath.

Feeling the pulsing and the warmth of her cum, deep inside of her pussy. Quickly brought him, racing to the heights of sexual satisfaction. His legs started to shake and his hips jerked as he himself started to cum and he began shooting deep inside of her.

Then with a loud moan and a few more slight jerks and thrusts, he filled her pussy to the brim. Now dripping wet, she soaked him as he pulled out.

"I told you I was man."

He said kissing her on the cheek,

"Yes you did and you sure are."

She said, as she picked up her robe and put it back on.

Just has headlights turned into the driveway.

"Better get yourself dressed quickly."

"Matt's home."

She said with a wink and she headed back to her room.

Mitch quickly got dressed, just in time for Matt to walk into the room.

"See."

"I told you, I wouldn't be long,"

"What did you do, while I was gone?"

Asked Matt.

"Oh nothing much."

"Just watched videos."

Mitch answered, tossing the controller at Matt.

"Let's play."

The mile high club

Boarding the plane and taking his seat. He couldn't help but stare in her direction. A beautiful stewardess, long blonde hair pulled back, stunning blue eyes and an ass he just wanted to bite.

As he got comfortable in his seat, an announcement came over the speaker.

"Ladies and gentlemen, the Captain has turned on the Fasten Seat Belt sign.

If you haven't already done so, please stow your carry-on luggage underneath the seat in front of you or in the overhead compartment. Please take your seat and fasten your seat belt. And also make sure your seat is back and folding trays are in their full upright position.

If you are seated next to an emergency exit, please read carefully the special instructions card located by your seat. If you do not wish to perform the functions described in the event of an emergency, please ask a flight attendant to reseat you.

We remind you that this is a non-smoking flight. Smoking is prohibited on the entire aircraft, including the lavatories. Tampering with, disabling or destroying the lavatory smoke detectors is prohibited by law.

If you have any questions about our flight today, please don't hesitate to ask one of our flight attendants."
"Thank you."

He wasn't even paying attention. Instead he sat there watching her, moving up and down the isle, helping passengers get seated,

He found himself wanting her. So fit and beautiful, he imagined everything he could do with a women like that.

Noticing him watching her, she asked,

"Sir, are you okay? "

"Is there something you need?"

He smiled a flirtatious smile as he responded.

"No I'm great beautiful."

"I'm Zander and you're?"

He asked.

She smiled.

"I'm Alexis."

"Enjoy the flight,"

She said headed to front for further announcements.

"Ladies and gentlemen, this is Melinda and I'm your head flight attendant. On behalf of Captain Anderson and the entire crew, welcome aboard Western Airlines flight 222 non-stop service from Toronto to New York City"

"At this time, we ask you to please make sure your seats are back and tray tables are in their full upright position and that your seat belt is correctly fastened. Also, your portable electronic devices must be set to 'airplane' mode until an announcement is made upon arrival."

"Thank you."

Zander, continued to watch her and each time she looked his direction, he winked and she would blush.

Totally intrigued by her, as he watched her running through the safety demonstration. Desperate to speak to her. He waited for her to finish then signalled for her to come over.

"Yes Zander."

She asked.

"We're almost ready to take off."

"Is there something you need?"

Before he could respond, the captain came back over the loud speaker.

"Flight attendants, prepare for take-off please."

"Cabin crew, please take your seats."

She put her hand on his shoulder.

"I'm sorry Zander, I'll see you as soon as we take off."

She said then rushed back to the front.

Frustrated he waited for the flight to take off. So he would be free to approach her and hoped he would get the chance.

" Ladies and gentlemen"

Another announcement echoed through the plane.

"The Captain has turned off the Fasten Seat Belt sign, and you may now move around the cabin. However we always we recommend you keep your seat belt fastened while you're seated."

"In a few moments, the flight attendants will be going around the cabin for those, who would like hot or cold drinks or snacks. Now, sit back, relax, and please enjoy the flight." "Thank you."

Now in the air, it was Zander's chance to make his move. He looked over to Alexis, who was chatting with Melinda at the front of the cabin. They seemed deep in conversation, so he waited for her come his way.

"Melinda."

"Did you see the guy in row 14, isle seat?"

Alexis asked.

Melinda raised her eye brows looking in his direction.

"Mhmm I sure did."

"Oh the things I could do to him."

She said with a laugh.

Alexis smiled biting her lip.

"I know, me too."

She said.

"Maybe he'd like to earn his mile high card."

Melinda said with a laugh.

Alexis laughed.

"Yea if only."

"I couldn't do that though."

She said.

Melinda smirked nudging Alexia's shoulder.

"Hell why not girl, you only live once."

"I say go for it, I'll cover for you."

Alexis smiled turning to look over at Zander, who was still watching her.

"True, you do only live once."

She said walking in his direction.

"Is there anything you need Zander?"

She asked, giving him a flirty smile.

He took her hand.

"Sure, I'd love a coffee, with a side of you."

He said, running his fingers up her arm.

She quivered with his touch as she smiled and gave him a wink.

"Well then."

She said.

"I have to finish serving drinks."

" and then, let me see what I can do about that."

He was shocked, yet at the same time excited. She hadn't given him the brush off. Instead she seemed interested in him.

She headed back up the front. Melinda immediately asked.

"So........."

"Are you going to go for it?"

Alexis shrugged her shoulders.

"I want to."

"I mean I REALLY want to."

"I just don't want to risk my job, if I get caught."

She said, making him a coffee.

Melinda, leaned into her.

"Ahh you'll be fine."

"I won't say a word and you know damn well. Anderson has given out a few mile high cards of his own. He won't do shit, if he finds out."

"I say go for it, I know I would."

Alexis smiled.

"Yea you're right about Anderson."

She said with a laugh.

"Better take him his coffee."

She walked back over to Zander, handing him his coffee.

"Your coffee Sir."

She said handing it to him.

Then she jotted something down on a piece of paper, handed to him and with a seductive wink she walked away.

Zander, opened the paper to see what she had written. The note read.

"Enjoy your coffee, then if you'd like to. Meet me in the lavatory in twenty minutes."

His heart started racing, not believing what he had just read, he read it again.

He looked over to her, to see her watching him, waiting on a reaction.

He winked and blew a kiss, then mouthed the words "See you soon."

She smiled and winked back.

Twenty minutes quickly passed and Zander headed to meet her. He stepped into the lavatory and waited. Seeing him go in, Alexis followed. Slipping inside without being noticed by any of the other attendants or passengers.

"Well hello there Sir."
She said putting her hand on his cheek, then running her fingers through his hair.

"Hello beautiful."
He replied while pulling her closer to him.

She quivered feeling his body against her. As she gently kissed his neck and licked his ear lobe.

She could feel his cock becoming hard in his pants, as it pressed against her leg.

"Mhmm….. is that for me?"
She asked, as she got down on her knees and unzipped his pants, freeing him to her gaze. She grabbed a hold of him and started stroking him up and down and then sliding him

into her mouth, she started sucking him. Pushing him deep into her throat, she stroked his balls with her hand. His legs shaking with the feeling of her warm lips wrapped tight around him.

His animal wilds now unleashed, as he took over and started ramming himself into her throat. Deep and hard, while holding her head against him. She gagged with each thrust, her eyes watered. He keep going harder and faster, her gagging sounds arousing him further.

His body shaking, ready to cum. He pulled out of her mouth, grabbed her by the hair and pulled her up. Then turning her against the wall, the lifted her skirt and pulled down her now moist panties. Then putting one of her legs up on the seat and bending her forward. He pushed his hard cock inside of her. At first slowly, teasing her with just the tip. Then pushing deeper, forcing a moan out of her. Then pulling back out and teasing her again.

Her pussy now soaked and aching for him.

"Give it to me Zander, give it to me."
She begged.

As he started pounding her hard and deep. Faster and faster, while reaching up into her blouse and pinching her nipples.

His cock so hard, her pussy so tight. He groaned and jerked with pleasure. She moaned as her breathing intensified and she started to cum, soaking his cock deep inside of her.

Feeling her cum, brought him racing to the heights of sexual satisfaction. Now ready to cum himself, He pulled out. Then pushing her down towards his cock. He quickly forced himself back into her mouth and started thrusting in and out of her throat. Faster and faster allowing his hot cum to spurt from his cock and right down her throat.

She tried to pull away, but he held her head tight to him, gagging her as she took in every drop.

Now getting up, she pressed her body against his. She kissed his cheek and whispered into his ear.

"Welcome, to the mile high club"

Lady of the night

Moonlit midwinter's night, she walked back and forth up the street. Her heel boots slipping on the ice, crisp snow crunching beneath her feet. She had been walking for hours.

Passing the time, until they met. her usual John, her secret meeting once a week.

She texted him, letting him know she was there, waiting on the street. He never left her out there for long, to be seen. Always rushing her inside.

She walked up to the door, but before she could knock. The door flew open and once again he rushed her inside. Unseen from anyone who may be watching.

Always a warm and inviting smile and eyes a girl could easily get lost in.

"Hello, I hope your week was a good one."
She said stepping inside.

Him closing the door, while she slipped off her snow covered boots.

"Yes it was an okay week."
"Much better, now that my special girl is here though."

He said putting his arm around her.
"Shall we?"

He asked pointing her in the direction of the spiral staircase that led to his room.

She turned hugging him tightly and kissed him.

"I've missed you and yes we shall."
She said hopping in front of him and heading up the stairs.

He followed behind, watching her ass as she moved up the stairs.

"Mhmm I'm loving the view."

He said, giving her ass a smack.

She jumped.

"Ooh, settle down now."

She said with a seductive giggle.

At the top of the stairs, rose petals led the way to his room.

"What's this?"

She asked.

"This is new."

She said turning to him.

He smiled kissing her sweetly.

"You're my special girl, it's been a year now. Since you started being the highlight of my weeks."

"I wanted to make today a little more special."

She wasn't sure how to respond. She never liked to get personal like that, with any of her johns.

"I see, very nice of you."

"You know though, that this is still just business don't you?"

She asked.

Putting his arm around her, he quickly responded.

"Oh yes, of course."

"Even in business, there's perks though."

He said with a wink.

She laughed and headed into his room. On the table, sat a bottle of champagne and two glasses and a fire burned in the fireplace. The lights were dim and there were more rose petals leading to the sofa in front of the fire.

"Wow!"

She said.

"I almost feel like pretty woman, here tonight."

He popped the cork on the champagne and started pouring.

"That's good, you should."

Then handing her a glass of champagne, he sat beside her on the sofa.

"Cheers, to a year of flawless rendezvous."

He said holding up his glass.

She smiled sweetly, clinking her glass to his.

"Yes cheers."

As they sat, sipping champagne and staring at the roaring fire. She listened, while he spoke of his family, his work and his troubles. For him, their weekly visits were more then just sex. He also enjoyed the companionship and just having someone to listen to him.

Sometimes he would talk for hours and others, only a few minutes. She never minded listening to him, even if it took all night. Because at the end of the night. He always made sure, she was well taken care of and then some!

Aside from talking, he always had a way about him. Particular likes and needs that were to always be met.

He leaned over and kissed her neck. Then whispered into her ear.

"Why don't you take it off."

"Stand up and give daddy what he likes."

Knowing exactly what he wanted. She stood up, right in front of him and slowly removed her clothes. Piece by piece seductively tossing them aside.

Then standing before him, completely naked. She started to dance, swaying her hips and twirling around, letting him see every inch of her.

Then she squeezed her breasts and leaned forward, allowing them to hang right in his face.

Then straddling his legs, she swayed back and forth. Her ass right in his gaze, her pussy waving right above his now hard cock.

He grabbed her ass hard, with both hands then leaned forward and bit her hard. She let out a small scream, but didn't stop. Swaying above him, enticing him, making him want even more.

He moaned, unzipping his pants. His cock now protruding from them. As he grabbed ahold and starting stroking himself. She turned around to face him. Pushing his face between her breasts. Shaking his head between them, then grabbing them. He squeezed them hard, then leaned in a bit one. Hard enough, his teeth marks were left behind. Then moving to her nipples. He sucked them, one by one. Then encircled them with the tip of his tongue.

Now so hard they ached. Her body wanting him.

As she started to grind her pussy on him. Faster and faster, in a circular motion, then twerking her ass.

Him now so hard, he could barely stand it.

"Fuck me.......fuck me now !"
He shouted out.

She turned her back to him and straddling his hard and ready cock. She pushed it inside of her.

Moving her hips, up and down. She slid his cock in and out of her pussy. She moved slow at first, then faster pushing him deeper each time. He moaned as he watched his cock moving in and out of her.

His body now sweaty, his muscles tightening, his body all hers. He leaned forward running his tongue up her back. Then grabbing her hips he helped her move faster and faster. Now so deep, he could feel the back of her pussy.

She moaned loudly her breathing out of control. She knew she was about to cum, her thrusting started to slow and she twirled her hips on his cock.

Feeling her start to cum, he let out a loud groan and rammed his cock hard into her pussy. He started to shake, his legs jerked below her as his cum started to flow.

"Yes yes, uhh uhh!"

"That's my girl."

He shouted out.

Then as she slid off of him, he slapped her ass.

"I want that next."

He said, pouring her another glass of champagne.

"But first we drink."

He said handing her the glass.

"Why thank you Sir."

She said with a wink, then sipped her champagne.

They sat watching the fire and sipping champagne still lost in the after glow. He never said much, just watched her, wanting more. He leaned over and kissed her shoulder, then slid down and a grabbed on to her nipple. His cock now hard again.

"On the bed, face down ass up."

He demanded.

She got up and walked over to bed. Then getting on her, knees. She put her face in the pillow and her ass up.

He came up behind her. First pushing his fingers into her pussy. Then moving to her ass. He pushed his fingers in and out, getting her ready for him. He moved closer, pulling her ass to him. Then started to push his cock inside, the tip so hard and swollen, it hurt. She bit on to the pillow, as a scream rained for her throat.

He pushed harder and harder nudging a little deeper each time. Until finally he was deep inside of her. Her ass wrapped tight around him, tears streaming down her face. Her ass hurt, it burned.

He started thrusting in and out. Pounding her so hard, she was losing control of her senses. She screamed with pain, uncontrollably. She tried to stop but the screams were forced from her body.

She tried to pull away, but he grabbed her hips and pulled her back. Pushing himself deeper and harder.

She gripped on to the pillows so hard, he could see the whites of her knuckles. Seeing this always aroused him further. As he moved faster and faster.

"Take it! Take it my little slut.!"

He shouted out.

His body convulsing out of control ready to cum. His thrusts now so hard, it was impossible to tell where one ended and the next began.

"Uhh……uhh yes!"

"I'm gonna cum…..uhh yes!"

He shouted out as he started to cum. Then pulling out of her ass. He shot right across her back.

"That's my girl."

He said smacking her ass.

"There's clean towels in the bathroom, for you to clean yourself up with."

He said, as he put his pants back on a downed a glass of champagne.

Getting up off the bed, her legs feeling like jelly. She grabbed her clothes and headed into the bathroom.

When she came back out, he was ready to walk her out.

"Here's your pay and little something extra."

He said, handing her a wad of cash.

"Wow!"

"Thank you."

She said, kissing him on the cheek.

He walked her to the door, then with one final kiss on the cheek. She walked out and disappeared into the cold dark midwinters night

Surprise visit

Music blasted through her apartment, as Lisa ran around cleaning and singing along.

Kind of bored, a Saturday evening with no place to go.

As she dusted the living room, she heard a knock at the door.

"I wonder, who that could be?"

She said, running to the door and looking through the peep hole.

"It's Katie!"

She said, throwing open the door to let her in.

"Hey beautiful, what brings you here?"

She asked both excited and confused to see her.

"I was in the neighbourhood and nothing to do tonight. So I thought I'd pop in."

She replied stepping inside

"I hope you don't mind. Did you have plans?"

Katie asked.

" Nope, no plans at all, and of course I don't mind."

"You're my best friend and more. You're always welcome here."

Lisa hugged her tightly and then kissed her on the lips.

She was wet and cold, her hard nipples pressed against her.

"Is it raining outside?"

Lisa asked.

"You're cold"

"Yea it was just starting to come down, when I got here."

Said Katie

Do you have a sweater I could borrow?"

She asked.

"Of course, go ahead into my room and help yourself to the closet."
Said Lisa.

"I'll make us a few drinks."

"Sounds fantastic."

Katie said kissing her on the cheek.

Lisa made them drinks then sat down on the sofa. Not long after Katie came out the bedroom.

"I wasn't sure what to put on and my clothes were soaked."

"How's this?"

She asked. Standing before Lisa in nothing but a long button down shirt, only buttoned half way up, her breasts popping out the top.

"Wow!"

"That is perfect!"

Lisa said, running her hand up Katie's leg and lifting the shirt. Just enough, to see her lace panties that just barely covered her firm tanned ass.

"I'm Just happy we wear the same size"

Katie said, joining Lisa on the sofa and picking up her drink.

"Damn girl!"

"You make one killer drink. This will warm me up quick."

She said as Lisa moved a little closer.

"I know other ways to warm you up as well."

Lisa said with a wink and seductive glare.

Katie smiled as she replied.

"I don't know what I've done to deserve you."

As a cool breeze hit her shirt and her hardening nipples could be seen poking out.

Lisa leaned in and kissed her, while reaching into her shirt to caress her hard nipples

"How does that feel?"

She asked.

Katie let out a small moan.

"Mhmm absolutely amazing."

She said pulling Lisa into her. Their soft lips touch, they kiss passionately. Katie's arms wrapped tightly around Lisa's waist, pulling her even closer. She kisses her neck and moves to her ear. He warm breath sending a sensation right through Lisa's body. Her nipples harden and she could feel her panties getting moist.

"I want you."

Katie whispered.

"I want you too."

Lisa whispered back, unbuttoning the shirt that barely covered Katie's firm sensual body.

Katie pulled her closer to her and kissed her again. Their tongues touch, they moan as they start the remove each other's clothes.

Katie then holding Lisa's face to hers, kissed her while her other hand ran down her back all the way to her tight luscious ass.

Then leaning her back on the sofa, Katie sat on Lisa's lap, straddling her. Their breasts pressed hard against each other. Their nipples teasing each other, as their breathing intensified and moans shoot from their mouths, as Katie runs her I tongue down Lisa's body followed by a trail of kisses.

Lisa's moans now driving Katie wild. Getting louder and more intense with the feeling of their nipples brushing against each other.

Katie taking charge.

"Lay down on your back."

She commanded.

Lisa willingly complied. Then as she lay their naked, her nipples hard and her pussy wet aching.

Katie crawled on top of her. Pressing their bodies together, as she grabbed on to Lisa's perky breasts and started massaging them and leaning in to tease her nipples with her tongue.   Lisa's back arched in reply and her eyes closed tightly, as moans shot from her throat.

"You're so beautiful."

Katie whispered.

Lisa smiled, then returning the pleasure she started doing the same to Katie. Her hands moving slowly, she teased her nipples, rolling them between her fingertips.

The two of them swept away with erotic pleasure.

Lisa sits up and begins to suck and nibble at Katie's nipples.

"Lisa, I want you. All of you."

Katie says, lost in the sensations of Lisa's warm breath on her nipples.

She stops and looks into Katie's eyes, as Katie lay her back on the sofa.

Then starts a trail of kisses right down her body to her hips. Then pressing her face in between Lisa's legs and running her tongue right down her inner thigh and back to her pussy, making her shutter and ready for more.

"Oh please!"

"I want you."

Lisa begged, as Katie moved in closer, her hot breath now warming Lisa's sweet pussy.

Moans now echoing through the room.

Katie's mouth finds Lisa's clit and she begins licking her.

Slowly at first, then as Lisa moaned louder, Katie became further aroused and started to lick faster. Even burying her tongue inside to taste her.

Lisa's moans excited Katie, as she licked faster and faster encircling her clit with her tongue. Lisa dripping wet as she started moving her hips and even grabbed on to Katie's head, holding it where she wanted her.

Now so close, ready to cum."

"Uh uh oh yes!"

"Oh yes Katie!"

Lisa shouted out, gasping to catch her breath.

"Uh uh I'm gonna cum."

She shrieked.

Katie reaching up, grabbed her nipples pinching them and twisting them between her fingers.

"Oh Katie, oh yes.....yes!"

Lisa cried out.

She licked faster and faster, Lisa's back once again arching in reply. Her pussy pressing hard against Katie's face as she grabs on to her hair. Gripping Katie's head tight, as she started to cum. Her hips now jerking, her body shaking. Cries of pleasure echoing through the room. As her cum filled Katies mouth and she continued licking tasting the juices of Lisa's desire.

"Oh yes that's it. You taste so good."

Katie said. As Lisa finished, then pulled up and kissed her sweetly. Tasting herself on Katie's lips.

"Mhmm,"

"Your turn."

Lisa said, changing positions with Katie.

Katie agreed, sliding back on the sofa. Already soaking wet and anxious to feel Lisa's tongue on her pussy. So horny now, she knew it wouldn't take long for her to cum.

Sliding in between Katie's legs. Lisa started to lick her pussy, encircling her clit with the tip of her tongue and pushing her tongue deep inside to taste her. Licking the tender soft sides deep inside of her pussy. While Katie writhed about moaning with pleasure.

"Uh yes! Omg yes!"

Katie shouted out

" eat my pussy eat it good!"

She shouted.

Hearing her words, Lisa moved faster then stopping. She rammed her fingers deep inside Katie's love soaked pussy. Deep and hard, so hard she forced a scream from Katie's throat.

Katie now, opening her legs wider. Allowing Lisa to go deeper and harder while continuing to lick her clit with her tongue.

"Mhmm you like that?"

Lisa pauses to ask.

"Yes! Oh God yes!"

Katie cried.

Lisa lifting her head for only a second, Katie grabbed it and pushed it back to her pussy.

"Don't stop, don't........stop uh uh oh Lisa."

Katie shouted, grinding her pussy in Lisa's face soaking it.

Katie's body now shaking, hard to catch her breath as her pussy starts to pulse and she cums and the cries of pleasure fill the room.

Lisa now licking faster, licking her clean. Then moving up, she kissed her sweetly on the lips.

Katie now sitting up, she once again lay Lisa back.

"We're not done, spread those beautiful legs."

She demanded, getting on top of her.

Then lifting one leg, she straddled her, so their pussies pressed hard together. Both of them dripping wet. Then supporting Lisa's leg with her shoulder, Katie started to scissor her.

Their pussies grinding hard together, their clits hard and caressing each other.

Both of them gasping to catch their breath as the waves of pleasure course through their bodies.

Lisa latched on to Katie's nipple with her mouth, biting it lightly. Katie grabbed on to Lisa's and pinched it hard sending her sailing into orgasm.

Her body shaking, convulsing with pleasure, as Katie too started to cum. Both of them crying out with pure pleasure. Their bodies sweaty and at the same time, soaked with sexual juices.

They held each other tight, their naked bodies pressed hard together. Staring each other in the eyes with a passionate glare.

Katie grabbed Lisa's face and kissed her. Long, burying her tongue in her mouth.

Lisa held her tighter and ran her fingers through her hair.

"Katie, you're amazing."

She said.

Katie smiled laying her head beside her on the sofa.

"You're not so bad yourself."

"How was that, for a surprise visit?"

Katie asked.

Lisa pressing her head against hers.

"It was a surprise of the best kind

Party Girl

The birthday party was well under way and the birthday girl Jessie, was having an amazing time.

Her friends had rented a huge beach house and put together a party so huge, it would go down in history.

Knowing Jessie like they did. Her friends had chosen a kind of Hollywood nights theme, all the glitz and glamour of Hollywood with a few surprises tossed in.

They had planned cocktails and music. Dancing and even a few drinking games in the mix.

The ladies all wore glamorous cocktail dresses, some with glitter, some low cut. Some even so tight. It was impossible to wear panties under them.

Jessie's dress was a short little black number. The chest cut all the way down to her belly button and sequence lined the trim. So tight she couldn't wear panties and so short it came just below her perfectly round ass.

Her shoes were black stilettos, that she had already kicked off, as she danced around the dance floor sipping her third margarita.

Her best friend Cindy, pulled her aside and whispered into her ear.

"I've planned a super special birthday surprise for you."

Jessie was intrigued.

"You did? What's that?"

She asked.

Cindy grabbed her arm leading her off the dance floor.

"Come with me."

Jessie was confused.

" Where are we going? What about the guests?

Cindy laughed nudging her.

"Oh they'll be just fine. Everyone is having such a good time and this my friend. Is well worth walking away for."

Now super anxious, to see what awaited her. Jessie went with her into a back room.

Entering the room, it almost looked like the back room of a strip club,

"What is this? What's happening?"

Jessie asked.

Cindy led her to a chair in the middle of the room.

"It's your own private show."

She said turning on some flashing lights.

"Private show, what? What kind of show?"

Jessie asked as the music started playing.

Cindy, smirked.

"You're about to find out. Sit back and enjoy."

She said leaving the room.

Jessie sat back in the chair, as music blasted around her and lights flashed.

Moments later he appeared. A sexy built beautiful man with washboard abs and an ass so perfect she could bite it.

He started dancing around in front of her. Ripping off his shirt and tear away pants. Now standing before her, in nothing but a tight little g-string

Moving his hips and moving to her, swaying above her lap. She reached out and grabbed his ass giving it a squeeze.

He fell to the floor then slid his body across it, coming up between her legs and spread them wide. His hot breath between her legs enticing her, as he pulled away again moving his body over her.

She felt her pussy getting wet, watching him. He poured water over his head allowing it to roll down his chest. She reached up and ran her fingers down his rock hard abs.

He winked, leaning in like he was about to kiss her. Only quickly moving up instead, breathing on her neck. His hot breath sent shivers down her spine and she let out a moan.

He slid his hands up her smooth legs, right to the top of her thighs, just inches away from her now soaked pussy. He looked her right in the eyes, his so deep blue she melted into them.

"Take me, take me, right here right now,"

She cried out.

He raised his eyebrows and bit his lip, still looking her in the eyes. Now straddling her lap and dry humping her. She grabbed his ass hard, squeezing it and pulling him closer to her. Leaning down she licked his lower belly just above his waste band.

His cock becoming visibly hard, right there in her gaze. She wanted to grab on to it with her mouth but held back.

She wanted him, she wanted him bad. Maybe It was the margaritas, maybe the fact she had been single for awhile, but her body ached to wrapped up with his.

She hiked up her dress, pantiless

Sitting there, she started to play with herself. Her pussy dripping wet as she pushed her fingers inside. He watched her as he continued to dance seductively around her.

"Do you like what you see?"

She asked winking at him, still playing with her pussy.

He never answered, instead dropped to his knees and once again crawled in between her legs, his face just above her pussy. She pushed her hips upwards, forcing her pussy closer to his face.

He smiled looking up at her then bit his lip with a growl.

"Do you want it?"

She asked.

"If you do, take it!"

Grabbing his head and pushing him closer.

Then without hesitation, he pushed his face to her pussy and started to lick her and nibble ferociously at her clit.

She squirmed, her back arched and legs spread further, inviting him inside. He pushed his fingers inside of her, first one, then two, then four and soon his fist. He pounded her pussy hard while licking and sucking her clit.

Her pussy now so wet it dripped, his faced soaked from her. She moaned as her body started to quiver. Ready to cum, she yelled out.

Yes, yes oh God yes!"

"Make me cum, make me.......... cum!"

He continued to go at her, hard and fierce. Her body shaking, her legs like jelly as she exploded into massive orgasm. All over his hand.

"Yes Uh oh yes!"

She screamed out.

"Fuck me.....fuck me now!"

She said turning around on the chair and pushing her ass against him.

His cock now so rock hard, he never denied her request. Instead he got got up behind her, and drove his cock deep into her pussy. Starting to pound her deep and hard.

She yelled out

"That's it, fuck me, fuck me hard!"

He moved faster and faster, driving himself deeper with each thrust. So deep it hurt, as she panted and moaned with a mix of both pain and pleasure.

As he continued to fuck her long and hard. He leaned down and bit her ass, so hard it left marks and she let out a squeal.

Grabbing her hips he pulled her harder to him. Then yanked her by the hair forcing her back to arch and forcing his cock deeper.

So deep inside of her, his cock so swollen and ready to explode. Her pussy once again starting to cum, as it pulsed tightening hard around him. He moaned loudly and she screamed with erotic pleasure. Hearing her screams and feeling her pussy cum all over his cock. Quickly brought him to the heights of sexual pleasure and he burst into orgasm. Quickly pulling out, his hot cum shot across her ass.

Then leaning down, he kissed her neck and whispered in her ear.

"Happy Birthday party girl."

Then he smacked her ass and got dressed leaving the room.

She was still lost in the after glow. So much so, it was as if she were drunk. It was definitely a birthday that would go down in history and one she would never forget.

As she went back out to join the party and yelled out.

"Woohoo, let's party bitches

Sexual favours welcome

"What else should I know about you John?"

She asked, as he fidgeted with hands, seemingly nervous.

"Well."

He answered.

"I would say a very important and common fact about me. Is that I would gladly accept sexual favors of any kind from any woman that owed me a payment, no matter how small.

"I see."

She said as John continued

"I would even take another man's woman as payment, if that is how he chose to pay his debt to me."

Shocked she asked.

"Do you do business this way often?"

"Well, being it's not exactly socially acceptable. I've unfortunately only received payment this way, a few times."

He answered, still fidgeting.

"Can you tell me about it?"

She asked.

"The first time it happened, it was with an old friend, lover actually. "

He explained.

"She was on the verge of losing her business and needed some immediate financial assistance."

He continued.

"I offered to help her save her business. She was desperate, so even though she knew of my fetish it didn't stop her, from coming to me."

"I see."

She said.

"So what happened next?"

She asked and he went on.

" I agreed to help her and when she said. She wasn't sure, how she could pay me back. I told her how she could pay me back without it costing her a dime."

"She had to think it over, but in the end. She was so grateful she agreed and asked what she could do."

"My first request, was a blow job and oh, I remember it so vividly"

"She was shocked by my request and stood silently for a few moments. I smiled at her and she knew I was serious. She looked away, almost ashamed, then looked me dead in the eyes and said.

"That's it right? Nothing more after that?"

I remember I let out a chuckle responding to her.

"Yes that's all, once I fuck that pretty throat of yours, you'll be done,"

"It was almost as if she was afraid. The seriousness of her eyes made me wild. I love the feeling of degrading the women paying me back. It's all a part of it for me."

Shaking her head, she looked up from her note pad.

"Why do you think that is John?"

She asked.

" I really don't know, but it really is a rush."

He said.

"I see. So do I dare ask,what happened next?"

She asked.

"You seem very intrigued. Maybe hearing this is a turn on for you."

John said with a chuckle.

She jotted something down on her note pad.

"I'm just doing my job John."

She said and he continued.

"Well okay."

"As you can probably guess, she owed a debt that needed to be paid."

He said.

"So I unzipped and pulled out my cock, then ordered her down on her knees. I was already hard, just from seeing the fearful look in her eyes."

"So she complied. She got down on her knees before me and started to lick my rock hard shaft. Her soft tongue only teasing me and bringing out my animal wilds. I pressed my cock to her lips and forced them open."

"Then she started to suck me, she sucked slowly not taking it all in, so I rammed it in hard and deep. She gagged and looked horrified, making me crazy."

"I grabbed her pulling her hair then forced her head to me hard and held it there. My cock right to that back of her throat as I started to pound her throat over and over. She gagged and her eyes watered so much, her mascara streaked her face. I kept going so hard she was gasping for air. I'd pop her off every few thrusts letting her catch her breath, then go right back to it."

"At this point she was crying and hurting but I didn't stop. I thrusted in and out of her mouth faster and faster until I burst into explosive orgasm."

Then I pulled out and shot my cum across her dirty little face."

"Then I zipped up and tossed her a rag and told her to clean herself up and be on her way. We were done."

"I see."

She said

"And doing this to women, doesn't bother you at all John?"

She asked, still jotting things down.

He laughed.

"No not at all, I totally get off on it. Like I said, it's a total rush."

She sat taking notes and seemed to squirm a bit. Noticing this John couldn't help but ask.

"Is this turning you on?"

"It is isn't it? You're squirming."

She looked John dead in the eyes.

"No John!"

"I told you it's my job."

He walked over to her and ran his hand from her cheek down her arm and she quivered.

"You are turned on! You want me."

He said.

Taking off her glasses and shaking her hair down. She replied.

"Okay fine!"

"Yes I want you John."

"I want you to take me, right here in my office."

John laughed

"If you want me, show me."

"Show me, how bad you want me."

He said as he watched the nervousness on her face.

She stood up unbuttoned her blouse, revealing her black lace bra that tightly held her perky breasts.

He pulled her to him.

"I want you to beg for me."

He said running his tongue up her neck to her ear and whispering.

"Take it all off, show me you want me and beg for it."

She shook with his words, shivers running down her spine. As she slipped out of her clothes piece by piece leaving them on the floor.

Then moving towards him completely naked, she pushed him down into the chair and straddled him.

Then leaning in, she whispered into his ear.

"I want you to fuck me, please fuck me John."

It wasn't enough for him, as he slid her off his lap to the floor.

"No, I want you to really beg."

"On your knees, look me in the eyes and beg for it, like you're begging for your life."

He demanded.

Knowing that demeaning women was what turned him on, she complied.

On her knees she crawled to him. Looked him deep in his eyes, with a scared yet almost shy look and she begged.

"Please, please fuck me. I want you. I want all of you."

Resting her chin on his knee.

"I'll do anything you want. Just take me, please!"

She said.

He grabbed her by the hair, yanking her head back. Then bent down, his hot breath on her neck as he whispered into her ear.

"Stand up and bend over the desk with your ass to me. I'm going to fuck that tight little asshole of yours."

She quickly got up from her knees, then bending over her desk, she nervously stood waiting for what came next,

He came up behind her, pushed the back of head, he face now pressed hard against the cold desk.

He ran his fingers down her spin, causing her to shiver. Then sliding his fingers down, he entered her pussy. He pushed three fingers inside of her, sliding them in and out, teasing her. She squirmed and moved her hips, feeling him fingering her so deep. Her pussy now soaking wet, she dripped. He went harder and faster, she moaned with pleasure wanting more.

She cried out.

"Make me cum, oh God...... please make me cum."

He moved faster and faster, while rubbing his thumb on her hard clit.

Her body shaking, her legs like jelly ready to cum.

He slowed down, forcing her to beg.

"No oh please don't stop, I'm so close. Please......... please don't stop."

He pulled his fingers out and slapped her soaked pussy hard. Ready to explode she could barely stand it.

"You'll cum when I say."

He said

Then taking his hand and wetting her ass with her pussy juices. He moved to her ass and slowly, slid his cock inside. He pushed it slow, while still teasing her pussy with his hand.

The tip of his cock, so swollen it hurt as he pushed harder forcing himself deeper. Her pussy now so sensitive, she was ready to burst.

Now all the way in her ass, he started thrusting fast and hard. She cried out with pain, gripping the edge of her desk. He moved faster and faster, her ass hurt but her pussy throbbed,

He put his hand to her clit and rubbed it hard, almost violently. Her pussy dripping and starting to pulse. He rammed himself harder into her ass. Tears now streaming down her face, screams of pain shooting from throat, quickly turned to screams of pleasure as she started to cum hard. Her pussy squirting, arousing him further. His thrusts so hard now, her ass felt torn but she didn't stop him.

"Take it, take you little slut."

He shouted out. As he himself was ready to cum.

He moaned loudly and grunted as his body jerked uncontrollably and he started to cum, filling her ass so full that it dripped before he even pulled out. Her ass so sore, his cum stung as he pulled out and stepped away from her.

It took a minute for her to catch her breath and stand up.

He smacked her ass and she let out a yelp.

"Now that's a therapy session I can handle."

He said with a wink.

Still trying to catch her breath.

She smiled.

"Yes, no charge for today John."

He laughed zipping up his pants.

"I knew I'd get to you, it is my way after all."

Unsure how to respond to that. She opened the door for him.

"Next week same time?"

Hi winked as he left.

"You bet, see you then

The Fuck shop

My business was a simple one. Knowing the needs of my mature clients, I could provide

them the best personal service, designed just for them I have to emphasize on personal.

My shop is a unique one. Catering to the sexual fantasies of. my patrons. A true fuck shop,

women and at times men came to me with their darkest fantasies,to make them happen.

Kind of like a party planning thing. I would plan their sensual rendezvous. They chose

the location, props if any and were descriptive with their needs, wants and deepest

desires. Some planned it as a surprise for their significant other and others had me hire a

stud or call girl to tame their wilds.

Women and men, from all over came to my shop. Some drove for hours just to have

their fantasies met. Some of them wanted role play, some wanted to experiment and dip

their toes in forbidden waters. Some wanted BDSM, some wanted a group some were

even looking to swing.

So many fantasies, so many needs all met through my fuck shop. Some people

protested my shop opening and others celebrated it , regardless of what others thought.

This shop was my passion and one I loved to share and besides that, there was no

denying. Sex sells and will forever be, one of the most sought after commodities.

The bell above the front door rang, I jumped up from the desk and walked out front.

"Good morning Jackie ."

I looked around but didn't see anyone. Suddenly she popped up from behind the rack of

vibrators.

"Oh there you are, good morning Becky. How are you today?"

I asked.

Picking up a pink rabbit vibrator she responded with a frustrated tone.

"I've been better!"

She said.

" I was right in the middle of my morning self care and my damn vibrator died."

"Oh no!"

I said.

"That's no fun."

Placing a pink rabbit and purple one as well on the counter.

She laughed.

"I'm doubling up this time!"

I winked at her ringing up her purchases.

"Good plan, always have a back up."

I said.

Then as she went to leave, she turned back.

"Oh Jackie"

She said.

"I need to come back in and talk to you soon. Ive been going through a bit of a dry spell with my hubby. As you can probably tell from my vibrator frustrations."

Listening to her, I could actually hear the frustration in her voice.

"I see."

I said.

"So are you thinking, you want to plan a fantasy night and spice things back up?"

I asked.

She sighed.

"Yes I think so."

She said.

"I'm just not yet sure what exactly I want."

I understood, but wanted to help.

"Understandable,"

I said

"If you're free later this afternoon, I have an opening. We can sit down with a coffee and go over the options and figure out your likes and dislikes. I'm sure the perfect plan can be made and get that spark relit and burning bright."

Becky, seemed a little reluctant.

"Hmm, yea.....I don't know..... hmm maybe."

She said.

"I kind of want to go for it, but I'm a little nervous."

Biting her lip nervously she continued.

"Oh you know what?"

"Let's do this, you only live once and if it awakens Wayne again then it's worth it,"

"What time are you free today?"

She asked.

"I have two appointments this morning, but I can see you at two o'clock. Does that work?"

I asked.

Turning to head out, she waved.

"Perfect, I'll see you at two."

When two o'clock rolled around, Becky was no longer nervous. Instead she was ready to plan her fantasy night.

She arrived at my shop and we went into the back room to chat. I grabbed us each a coffee and we sat down.

"Have you thought of exactly what you would like? "

I asked.

"Did you want Romance, kink, a bit of both?"

"Have you thought of the location? At home, a hotel? Tell me your thoughts."

I said.

Becky handed me a sheet of paper, she had made notes on.

"Here's my ideas, just hoping you can find a way to spice that up a bit."

Reading over her notes, I was sure I could make the night amazing for her.

"Yes, I can definitely work with this."

"So we're doing this at home then? You know I can do you one better."

"You can?"

She asked.

"How?"

I continued.

" I have a penthouse apartment, we use all the time, for sexy photo shoots for clients and people wanting some glamour in their fantasies."

"Have you thought of a pole dance? You mentioned sexual dancing There's a pole in the penthouse."

I asked, showing her photos.

She was intrigued.

"I love it!"

She said with a huge smile.

"You can set it up just like I asked, with the candles and the music."

"I'll need the leather corset and panties do you sell them here? and the pole is perfect. Wayne is going to die."

She was overly excited, I could barely get a word in.

"Yes, I'll set it up perfectly and we do have the corsets here, so you can pick one out and I'll make sure it's there for you."

I explained

"Now, is this your fantasy? Or his that you're doing for him?"

I asked and she continued.

"It's his. He's always said he'd love to see me dressed in a leather corset and dancing seductively for him. I just never had the nerve before now."

"I see, well okay then."

I said.

"When are you thinking? I'd need at least a couple of days. Friday night work? I'd set it up and give you the keys. Then you can have him, meet you there. You'll have the place for the entire night."

Becky was thrilled.

"Oh my gosh, that's perfect and yes Friday is great. I'll leave it all up to you now and see you Friday for the keys."

She said with a huge smile.

"Yes, say around three on Friday."

"The keys will be here at the front counter for you and everything will be set for your perfect night."

 I said walking her out.

Friday quickly rolled around. I had everything all set for Becky to have a totally erotic and sensual night with Wayne.

She picked up the keys from me along with her corset and headed out to the penthouse.

Arriving at the penthouse, walking in. She ran into the care taker, I had warned her would be there until she arrived, taking care of last minute details.

Becky was astonished at how amazing it was. It was like something, right out of glamour magazine. In the bedroom, there was a gorgeous California king bed with black and red satin sheets. In the corner, a gorgeous stone fireplace where a blazing fire burned. There were candles on the mantle and around the room. Soft sensual music played and right in the middle of the room, facing the bed, was the stripper pole.

On the table there was champagne on ice and two glasses along with a bowl of fresh strawberries, chocolate sauce and whipped cream.

Becky slipped into her leather corset and panties and spike black thigh high heel boots and waited for Wayne to arrive. He had no idea what was about to happen, or even why he was to meet her there.

Then there was a knock at the door. She was excited but at the same time nervous.

"It's open."

She called out and Wayne walked in.

"Becks..... his nickname for her. Becks where are you?"

He asked.

She walked out into the hallway where he could see her.

He was shocked.

"Whoa Becks!"

He said, as she signalled to him to follow her.

"Mhmm You look amazing."

He said with a growl, following her into the bedroom.

"Wow look at this place,"

He said looking around.

Becky placed her finger over his lips.

"Shh, just enjoy my love."

Then slowly unbuttoning his shirt, she kissed he chest and slid it off. Then unzipping his pants, she let them fall to the floor and backed him into the bed, sitting him down on the end.

"Mhmm baby."

He said trying to kiss her.

She stopped him again putting her finger to his lips.

"Not yet baby, just enjoy,"

Wayne super intrigued and also getting hard with the anticipation of what was coming. Moaned, then kissed her finger pressed against his lips, as if to say okay,

Becky teasing him, bent down. Her breasts poking out the top of her corset right in his face. She kissed him, forcing her tongue into his mouth, then pulled away.

Then on her knees, she ran her tongue down his inner thigh, all the way down to his calf and then right back up, stopping just inches from his balls.

He quivered reaching out for her. His cock now rock hard.

Again she stopped him while continuing to tease him. Moving towards his cock, she pressed her face to him. Her hot breath on his balls, causing him to squirm.

"Mhmm I want you Becks, I want you now!"

He said reaching for her.

Shaking her head no as she bit her lip and gave him

A seductive glare.

"Not yet baby….. not yet."

Becky grabbed a strawberry off the table, covered it in whipped cream and fed to him, then kissed him lips licking off the extra whip cream. Then seductively walked away and over the stripper pole. She spun around the pole and slid up and down it. She gave him a pole dance he wouldn't soon forget.

Then standing before him, she removed her corset and panties and dropped them on the floor. Now completely naked, in nothing but her thigh high heel boots. She moved towards him.

His cock now so hard, he dripped.

As she lay him back on the bed. Then taking the whipped cream, she sprayed it on his nipples and down his belly to his cock. She licked it off little by little, driving him wild. Her tongue all over his body, teasing him as he squirmed beneath her.

Then moving to his cock, she pushed him into her mouth and started to suck him. Moving up and down his shaft while stroking the base with her hand. He squirmed and shook with pleasure as she pushed him right to the back of her throat causing herself to gag. She moved faster and faster, his cock now so hard it throbbed. He moaned with pleasure, his body started to jerk. Then right as he was about to cum, she stopped.

"No yet baby, not yet."

She said.

As she climbed on top of him and slid his cock deep into her pussy and started riding him, pushing him deeper and harder as she moved her hips wildly above him.

"Yes oh God yes!"

Wayne yelled out as she moved faster and faster.

He reached up and grabbed her breasts giving them a squeeze, then rolling her nipples between his fingers and giving them a pinch she moaned.

Now moving her hips in a circular motion, his cock so deep inside of her. Her pussy soaked and ready to burst. She moved faster, so fast his body shook and jerked. He was ready to cum, she was ready to cum. Their bodies as one, cries of pleasure filling the room. Her body now shaking, her pussy pulsing as she started to cum. Him feeling her cum all over his cock started to cum himself.

"Oh my God Becky! Oh my........God!"

He yelled out.

Her panting uncontrollably trying to catch her breath as she kept riding him through their explosive orgasms.

Then as she pulled off of him. Wayne decided he wasn't done with her. He grabbed the whip cream.

"Lay back,"

He said.

"I'm not done with you."

Then spraying whip cream across her pussy, he leaned in and started wildly licking it off. Her pussy so sensitive she squirmed and writhed about. He held her hips and nibbled ferociously at her. She moaned, his head buried deep between her legs as he kept going licking faster and faster.

Her body so overcome with pleasure? She cried out.

"Oh yes! Yes don't stop. Don't..... stop!"

Her pussy throbbing and dripping as he sprayed more whip cream and kept going wild at her.

Her clit so hard it ached as he latched on and sucked it hard. Her body now shaking uncontrollably on the brink of another orgasm.

He took his fingers and rammed them deep inside both her pussy and her ass at the same time. She let out a loud squeal, her body now almost convulsing as she started to cum.

He went harder and faster fingering her, causing her orgasm to linger longer. Her breathing now so rapid it was hard to catch her breath.

"Oh God, oh G........od!"

She cried out.

Her legs like vibrators around his head as he slowed down. Then pulling away, she lay almost breathless before him.

"I just wanted to give a little something back,"

He said, laying beside her.

She sat up.

"Well thank you for that."

She said kissing his forehead.

"Boy am I dehydrated."

"Join me for some champagne!"

She said tapping his leg.

"Lead the way my dear."

He said smacking her ass as she got up.

Then they sat by the fire, sipping champagne in the after glow. Their passion and desires for each other once again ignited.

Co- workers husband

It had been a super long week at the office and an even busier day.

Being an office manager, I had a lot of the work that was put on me and I was exhausted.

What I really needed was a shower and a chance to refresh, before an important meeting in just a few hours.

Unfortunately there was no possible way. I lived too far from the office and there just wasn't enough time to go home and still make it back in time.

One of my colleagues and a friend in the office, could see my frustration.

"Everything okay Jane?"

She asked.

Frustrated almost falling asleep on my feet I answered.

"Ah yea it's all good. I just really need a shower to wake me up, before the big meeting."

I said.

"But it's just been so busy today, there's not enough time left for me, to make it to the other end of town and back. With the traffic, it would take hours."

"Oh I see,"

Said Maria.

"You know Jane, my apartment is in the building right next door."

"I don't think Mark is home from work yet, you could run over and grab a shower there if you'd like"

I jumped at the chance for a hot shower.

"Really?"

I said.

"That would be fantastic. Are you sure you don't mind?"

She handed me her keys.

"No not at all. It's unit 206, go ahead. I'll hold down the fort here."

She said.

I gladly took the keys, then grabbed my bag.

"Thank you so much Maria, you're a lifesaver."

I said putting on my jacket,

"No worries at all."

She replied.

"There's wine in the fridge, have a drink and take a minute to relax if you'd like."

I really liked the sound of that.

"Fantastic, I owe you one girlie!"

I said as I rushed out.

I arrived at her apartment, it was an elegant little place. I took a quick look around to find the bathroom and headed in to the shower.

The shower was huge, it took up over half the room. Nicely tiled and a powerful very large rainfall shower head.

So relaxed as the hot water poured down On my body. I started to play with myself.

I squeezed my breasts and played with my nipples now hard as I rubbed them. Then reaching down between my legs, I started to caress my pussy. Then pushing my fingers inside, I started to finger myself. My clit now hard and needing attention. I encircled it with my fingertips. My pussy so wet, the hot water raining down on me, so relaxed yet so

aroused. My pussy now tingling, my legs feeling like jelly as I pressed my body against

the shower wall.

Then fingered myself deep and hard while pinching my nipples with my other hand.

Going at myself faster and faster then rubbing my clit almost violently until finally, my

body was taken over by erotic pleasure and I started to cum.

Now gripping on to the shower wall, my breathing intensified as I continued to rub my

pussy until I was so sensitive I couldn't cum no more.

Then I finished my shower, now completely relaxed. I got out and wrapped myself

in a towel.

Remembering Maria had mentioned wine, I went and poured myself a glass. Then sat

down on the sofa to enjoy it, still in nothing but a towel.

On the coffee table, I found the stereo remote and turned on some music. I still had time,

so took it to relax a while longer.

I wasn't able to hear anything else in the apartment over the music. So I hadn't

heard the door.

There I sat, naked in just a towel, my hair still wet, sipping wine, lost in the music.

When suddenly, I felt hands on my shoulders and someone kissed my neck.

"You're home early darling."

He said.

So startled, I jumped up from the sofa and so quickly, my towel fell to the floor.

There I was, standing completely naked my nipples hard from the cold air. In front

of Maria's husband Mark.

"Oh my God!"

I said totally embarrassed.

"I'm so sorry."

I said picking up my towel from the floor and wrapping it back around myself.

"Maria said I could come by and have shower and relax before our big meeting. I'm so sorry, I'll get out of your way."

I said rushing to go grab my clothes.

Mark followed me to the other room.

"Jane wait, it's okay."

"Come finish your wine,"

"I just wasn't expecting it to be you and from behind with your hair wet, you looked like Maria."

Still embarrassed I turned to him.

" this is so embarrassing."

I said.

"I'm in nothing but a towel, I didn't want my wet hair to drip on my work clothes and then show up at the meeting in wet clothes."

I said cinching they towel tighter.

Mark put his hand on my shoulder, in almost a flirty way.

"You have nothing to be sorry for, now come on,"

"Join me in a glass of wine, before you have to leave."

He said grabbing my arm.

"I think I should put my clothes on first, don't you?"

I asked.

He smiled and winked as he responded.

"Umm no why?"

"You don't want to get your clothes wet and you're covered up. It's all good, come on and join me."

Then as we walked back into the living room, he said with a chuckle.

" besides, I've seen it all now anyway."

So embarrassed I laughed.

"Yes I suppose you have."

We sat on the sofa drinking wine together, music still playing. Mark cracked jokes and kept staring at me, almost as if he was still picturing me naked.

He was a gorgeous man and so built his eyes were like blue crystals that sparkled when he look at you. Maria was a very lucky women and I admit I was a little jealous.

As I sat eyeing him up, hoping he wasn't noticing. He suddenly slid closer to me and put his hand on my knee.

"You're a very beautiful woman Jane."

He whispered in my ear, sending shivers down my spine.

I shuttered with his touch as he started to stroke my knee and slide his hand upward and under my towel.

"Mark, what are you doing? You're Maria's husband."

He continued sliding up my towel.

"Yea, but come on Jane. I've seen the way you look at me when ever I'm around. I know you're attracted to me."

I couldn't deny it, he was absolutely gorgeous and it had been so long since I'd been with a man.

"Well yes that's true, but you're my friends husband and not just friend. I work with her every day."

I said sliding his hand away.

He leaned down and started kissing my bare shoulder.

I quivered in response, it felt so good.

Then he slid his fingers down the top of my towel and in between my breasts.

I was melting, yet trying to fight off of urge.

"Come on Jane, just one and done. Nobody has to know."

He whispered.

"I feel you wanting it."

He said loosening my towel and it opened up.

Trying to fight it, I attempted to pull my towel back up, but he kissed my neck and his warm breath when he got my ear, did it and I was done for. Losing control of my senses I gave myself to him, I kissed him and then let him have his way with me.

He leaned in and grabbed on to my hard nipples with his teeth, giving them a gentle bite. Then rolled his tongue over them and down my body, he stopped at my pussy. He lifted my legs on to the sofa forcing me spread eagle and started to tease and lick me. He encircled my clit, my pussy now dripping wet as he shoved his tongue deep inside of me. Twirling it around over and over.

Then pulling his tongue out he ran it up my body, all the way to my neck, then right back down. Only stopping at my pussy for a brief second then he rolled it down my inner thigh.

My body was quivering with his touch.

I wanted him, I wanted him inside of me.

Reaching down I grabbed on to his cock. It was hard and seemed huge. My pussy throbbed with the very thought of him pounding me with it. I stroked him up and down and caressed his balls. Him now back at my pussy, he shoved his fingers inside and teased me deep inside. Then rubbing my clit hard with his thumb. My body began to shake, knowing I was on the verge, he pulled his fingers out and pushed his tongue in, to taste my cum now filling my pussy as it pulsed and I cried out with pleasure.

"Atta girl."

He said.

"You taste delicious, cum some more for me."

He demanded still rubbing my clit hard and fast.

My body convulsed my orgasm lingering and then just as it started to finish another one started.

"Oh my God, uhh, uhh, "

I cried out, my legs now tight around his head,

Him licking faster and faster.

"Mhmm yes, yes, you cum so good."

He shouted out.

Then smacking my thigh, he told me to roll over with my ass in the air.

"Come on, over you go."

"Face down, ass up. I want to fuck that cute little button hole of yours."

Nervous knowing how big he was, yet wanting him so badly. I quickly complied with his request.

I turned over with my face to the couch cushion and pushed my ass towards him.

I felt him come up behind me, nervous I clenched the cushion.

Then spreading my ass cheeks apart, he spit on my ass. Then started to slid himself inside. He was so big and so hard, he barely had the tip in and it already hurt. I let out a loud groan of pain, my face now pushed hard into cushions trying to muffle my cries.

He pushed harder and harder, inching in bit by bit. My ass hurt, he was too big. I wasn't sure I could handle it, but yet I didn't stop him.

I screamed out in pain, my cries seemed to arouse him further. Then with one super hard push, he was in. In me so deep I could barely breath. My ass was on fire as he started thrusting hard and fast, in and out of me. Cries forced from my throat, tears streaming down my face. He was going wild, pounding me and groaning with each thrust. It hurt but at the same time I enjoyed it. My body was all his, In and out In out so hard and deep.

I could feel is cock swelling further, the more aroused he got. Filling my ass so tightly, his body starting to shake. His breathing now quicker and groans louder. I knew he was about to cum as I shouted out.

"That's it cum for me, fill my ass with your cum."

He let out a loud grunt and started to jerk as his cum spurted from his cock deep inside my ass.

"Yes, yes!"

He yelled out ramming his cock one last time and then leaning down and biting my ass cheek.

He slowly pulled out, and stood up.

My ass hurt so badly his cum dripping from me burned.

"How was that for relaxing?"

He asked as I stood up.

I smiled kissing his cheek.

"That's one way to get rid of tension, no doubt there."

He laughed pulling his pants back up and I quickly got dressed.

He rubbed my cheek.

"You better quickly fix your makeup."

He said and ran into the bathroom to fix myself up.

"I've got to hurry."

I yelled out.

"The meeting is in fifteen minutes"

Then running out, I kissed his cheek.

"Thank you, for the stress relief."

He laughed.

"You're welcome, now go!"

I ran out and back over to the office. Walking in Maria was waiting.

"There you are, I was worried you'd fallen asleep over there."

I laughed.

"I actually did, but lucky for me, I woke up on time. Now let's get to the boardroom

My best friends father

Allie, quickly packed a bag, excited for a night away.

Jill her best friend since the fifth grade, was home from college for the weekend. The girls hadn't seen each other since graduation. They had tried to get into the same college, but only Jill got in. Allie had to settle for the small community college here at home.

She was desperate to see Jill, it had been what seemed like forever. She picked up her phone and shot off a quick text to her.

"Hey girlie, are you on the way?"

She quickly checked her makeup and took one more look to be sure She had everything She needed.

She was bouncing with anticipation and couldn't wait to hear, more about her life in a big city and attending an Ivy League college.

Since Jill left, Allie felt almost trapped. Stuck in their tiny home town with only one small community college. Nothing big and exciting like what Jill landed.

She also couldn't wait to hear about the guy Jill had met and had been secretly fooling around with for weeks.

Allie sat on the steps, waiting on Jill to arrive. She was so overly excited, she anxiously tapped her foot.

Suddenly a horn honked in the driveway. She was here, or so Allie thought. As she walked out to the car, she noticed it was Jill's father.

He stepped out of the car and helped her with her bag and she slipped into the back seat. Just as she got in, a text came in from Jill.

"Hey girlie, sorry I forgot to warn you. My father offered to pick you up. Can't wait to see you!"

Allie sent a quick text back as Jill's father got back into the car.

"No worries see you soon."

Then looking up, she noticed Jill's father watching her in the rear view mirror and their eyes met.

"You've really grown up Allie, not the little girl I remember."

He said.

"You and Jill both have, time sure goes by fast."

She agreed, even though for her it felt like time was dragging.

"Yes we're definitely not little girls anymore sir."

She said.

"Allie, I've told you before. You can call me Tim. Sir makes me feel old, sir's my father."

He said with a laugh.

She had been raised to always call people by Sir, Ma'am or Mr. or Mrs. never by their first name. So calling Jill's father Tim, just never came naturally to her.

"I know, I'm sorry I'm just not used to that so I forget."

She said

Still glancing at her in the rear view mirror every so often, he smiled with a wink.

"Well okay, from now on then. It's Tim."

He said and she agreed.

They pulled into Jill's driveway and as soon as Allie got out of the car, Jill came running out.

"ALLIE."

She shrieked running up to her and hugging her.

Both of them excited to be together again.

"Oh my God girl, I have so much to tell you"

Jill said as they headed inside. Jill's father grabbed her bag and brought it in.

"I'll put Allie's bag in your room Jill."

He said.

"Okay thank you Daddy."

"We'll be right up."

She said, taking Allie into the kitchen.

"Come on, we're going to need snacks and drinks."

"Grab what you like."

She said.

Now with their arms full of snacks and drinks they headed up to her room,

passing her father in the hallway.

"Boy this brings back memories."

He said with a laugh,

Jill agreed.

"Yes, just like the good ole days, with my bestie."

The girls headed into Jill's room.

"Girl, I am so happy to see you ."

Allie said.

"You haven't missed anything here at home. Same old same old, boring small town, same

guys never anyone new. Even at school, it's just all the same people."

"So tell me about your school. What is it like living in a big city?"

She asked.

"Well, to be honest living in a big city isn't all that great, it's always busy and loud and everything is more expensive."

Jill explained.

"What about the people? I bet there's a lot of great people there and probably a ton of amazing guys."

Allie asked and Jill continued.

"Seriously no, I mean I'm sure there are great people in the city, but at my school. So far I've only met pompous rich kids, that think everyone else is beneath them. As for guys, so far most have been total asses with the rich Mama's boy attitude. The only one I've really liked, Is Charlie."

She said.

Allie had been waiting to hear about Charlie.

" Oh yea Charlie, tell me about him."

Said Allie.

"There's not really much to tell, we've only been seeing each other for a few weeks. He's super cute though and we really seem to click."

Jill explained, just as her father came to the door.

"Dinner is ready ladies, taco night."

The girls headed down stairs for dinner, where Tim sat right across from Allie and just like in the car, he stared at her when ever he thought she wasn't looking.

Allie never really minded. I mean Tim was a very good looking man, but she still couldn't help but wonder why he was always watching her.

After dinner, the girls decided to go watch a movie in the den and Tim came in to join them.

Allie was finding it strange that Tim was hanging around them so much, but at the same time flattered with the way he looked at her.

About half way through the movie, Jill left to go the washroom. Allie rubbed her neck, that was a little stiff.

"Stiff neck Allie?"

Tim said sliding over next to her. Then starting to rub her neck.

"I can fix that for you."

He said, now so close she could feel his warm breath on her shoulder.

"You've grown into a very beautiful woman."

He whispered.

Allie shivered with his words, whispered in her ear.

"Thank you Tim."

She quietly replied.

Then hearing Jill headed back, he gently ran his hand down her cheek and pulled away.

The rest of the movie, was filled with stolen glances and grins, even winks. Between Allie and Tim.

She found his interest in her intriguing and she was anxious to see where it led. She has always found Tim attractive and as a young girl even had a crush on him. She used to imagine being older and him being her husband or boyfriend.

The way he watched her, gave her chills and made her heart race. She found herself wanting him, but did he want her?

After the movie, Jill was exhausted.

"I'm done."

She said.

"Time for bed, goodnight Daddy."

"Are you ready Allie?"

She asked.

"Ah yea sure. Let's go."

She said glancing back at Tim giving him a wink.

Jill scooted up the stairs and Allie lagged behind.

"I'll be up a while longer Allie."

"Just in case you need anything,"

He said giving her a seductive glance.

She winked and bit her lip, then headed up the stairs.

The girls chatted for a bit, but Jill quickly fell asleep. So Allie decided to sneak back downstairs and see what Tim was up to.

It was dark and at first she didn't see him. He was over in his lazy boy, sitting with headphones on listening to music. She was afraid to startle him, so she turned on a lamp in hall, so he would see it come on and know she was there.

"Allie."

He said.

"I was hoping you'd come back, come join me."

He said patting his lap.

She walked towards him and reached out grabbing her arm, then pulling her to him, he sat her on his lap.

He ran his fingers through her hair and then down her back, stopping at her hips. She shivered with his touch, her heart raced.

"Tim."

She said.

"You're my best friends father."

"Yes Allie I am."

He replied

"But you're an adult now and there's really nothing wrong with it."

He said leaning in and gently kissing her neck.

She quivered as her breathing changed and she turned to kiss him back.

Putting her hands on his face, she pulled him close and kissed him long and passionately, their tongues in each other's mouths.

He hurriedly slipped off her shirt and started caressing her perky little breasts. Her nipples so hard, they could cut glass.

She moved to his neck and ran her tongue up it and then nibbled at his earlobes. He moaned as chills went down his spine. His cock now rock hard in his boxer shorts and protruding out the top. Reaching down, she took him into her hand and started to stroke him up and down. Then sliding down on to the floor and in between his legs. She started to lick his rock hard shaft. Running her tongue up and down, then moving to his balls, she sucked them gently.

He was now so hard his cock throbbed as she moved to the tip and started to suck him. Pushing him deep into her throat. In and out in and out, popping off at the tip only to tease him further with her tongue. She moved faster and faster, his cock so swollen it filled her mouth. He pushed her head forcing himself deeper. She gagged as he held her there, then pulling her hair he ripped her off of him. She gasped catching her breath.

"Lay on your back."

He demanded getting down on the floor.

She lay on her back, he quickly pulled off her pyjama pants. Then spreading her legs he lifted her feet on to his shoulders and moved towards her. Pushing his rock hard shaft deep into her pussy. Not yet wet, he went in dry, pushing in just the tip and then with one hard thrust. He rammed himself all the way in deep and hard. She let out a scream as his cock pounded the back of her pussy. Then as he started thrusting hard and fast in and out of her, she arched her back and moaned. Her pussy now wet and throbbing as he filled her. His deep thrusts hurt as she let out subtle cries. Leaning down he bit her hard nipples and teased her with his tongue. Her body overcome by pleasure and heightened arousal but the thought they could get caught.

She squirmed below him, her legs on his shoulders shaking. Him groaning as he started to peak.

"Oh yes Allie, yes!"

"Take it baby girl, take it!"

He said in a raspy voice almost growling. His body completely taken over and ready to cum.

She moaned loudly, her hips now jerking as her pussy started to pulse. She grabbed on to his ass and pushed him harder to her. Feeling her ready to cum, he pushed even harder, now so deep it hurt and tears filled her eyes.

"Oh my God."

She shouted

"I'm going to cum….. uh uh yes!"

She moaned.

Hearing her words drove him wild, his body now starting to jerk, his legs shaking.

"Oh yea, yes, yes."

He groaned as he himself started to cum. Her pussy now pulsing hard around his cock, tightening so hard as his cum shot deep inside of her.

The two of them writhing about in pure ecstasy, their cum mixing together deep in her pussy.

Leaning down his kissed her nipple, now so overly sensitive she shuttered.

"Oh my God."

She said

"That was amazing."

He agreed pulling out and away from her. Her pussy still throbbing, she dripped as she got up from the floor.

He kissed her on the forehead.

"Thank you beautiful."

She smiled looking him in the eyes.

"I guess I should get back upstairs so we don't get caught."

He agreed smacking her ass.

"Yea I guess so, until next time then?"

She winked and blew him as kiss and was gone

Maid by the hour

Finishing up in a room, I was asked to report to the housekeeping office. It seemed the occupant of the penthouse room, was looking for a full time maid to be paid by the hour.

He had a specific look in mind and apparently I fit the bill.

Tall, long blonde hair baby blue eyes and a perfectly fit body. Oh and according to my boss, making it very awkward. I had the perfect sized breasts and nice round ass.

"Umm I see."

I said.

"What kind of maid is he looking for exactly?"

I asked.

My boss seemed frustrated with my question.

"Do you want the job or not?"

"You'd have to see him today and be approved. He's a very private person and particular about who he has around."

I was intrigued by the opportunity yet still unsure.

"Is the pay the same?"

I asked.

My boss still awaiting my answer quickly responded.

"No actually, he's willing to pay triple for the right girl."

Hearing that, there was no more need to think about it.

" I'll take it!"

I said jumping up.

"When do I meet him?"

I asked.

My boss handed me a folder with instructions and rules for this man's potential maid "Go and fix yourself up and head up there. I'll let him know, you'll be there in 30 minutes."

I agreed and headed out. Going over the rules, there were specifics listed. Like I had to always to look a certain way. Make up and hair done. Short uniform that was to be no longer then the bottom of my ass and he insisted she maid wear a thong. These were very odd requests and I couldn't help but wonder what I had gotten myself into.

I quickly fixed my hair and makeup, put on a thong and slipped into my smallest uniform, so small it barely covered my ass and the bottom of my cheeks peeked out of the bottom. Then I headed up to the penthouse.

I was nervous, my heart pounded. Who was this man, with such demands of his maid.

I arrived at the penthouse and quickly pulled myself together, before knocking on the door. I couldn't appear nervous, I needed to exude confidence.

I knocked on the door and waited.

Moments later it opened and there before me stood one of the sexiest men I'd ever seen. Beautiful chiselled face with the perfect smile and dimples. Amazing blue eyes so deep It was if I could see into his soul. Perfect hair and a body and ass to die for.

I swear, just standing there, I could feel my pussy getting wet and my nipples standing at attention.

He looked me up and down and spun me around.

"Perfect, you'll do just fine."

"Have you read my rules?"

He asked.

I nodded stepping inside.

"Yes Sir I have."

I said.

He led me into the apartment.

 "What exactly, did your boss tell you about the position?"

He asked.

"He really never told me much, just that you needed a maid to be paid by the hour and what the pay was."

I answered.

He explained.

"Yes, the job comes with a few perks to go with that hefty pay cheque. As long as you're willing to comply."

I was confused.

"Perks, what perks?"

I asked as he pulled me close to him, kissed my neck and whispered.

"The sexual kind."

A shiver ran down my spine and I swear my pussy tingled hearing those words. I was single and the thought of this beautiful man pounding my pussy almost drove me wild.

"Are you still in?"

He asked, running his fingers down my cheek.

I shivered with his touch.

"Yes, yes sir I'm in."

He smacked my ass, his fingertips catching the bottom of bare cheeks.

   I jumped.

"Ooh!"

I said with a giggle.

He led me to the sitting room.

"This room could use a good dusting. Be sure to bend down and get in all the corners, I'll just sit here and watch."

He said and I quickly got to work. Reaching and bending. Revealing my ass and cleavage to him each time. He sat on the sofa watching me. Apparently watching his maid clean in skimpy clothes aroused him, because when I glanced over. His hand was in his pants and he was stroking himself.

Seeing him getting so aroused by me.

I bent down, wiggling my ass enticing him further.

Then reaching into the corner, I felt him come up behind me.

"I think you missed a spot."

He said grabbing my ass hard with his hand.

"I did? Where?"

I asked.

"Right here."

He said pressing his hard cock to my cheek.

Then grabbing me by the hair, he turned my head and forced his cock into my mouth. I was surprisingly aroused by his forcefulness, as I happily started to suck his cock. My pussy getting wetter with each thrust of his cock into my mouth. My nipples so hard, they could be seen through my blouse. I continued to suck him, taking him all into my mouth. So deep I gagged myself when it hit the back of my throat.

I moved faster and faster, grabbing the base of his shaft with my hand. Then moving to his balls, I pushed them into my mouth and gently sucked them teasing them with my tongue. His legs shook, my pussy throbbed wanting him inside of me. As I continued to go at him faster and faster now pushing him back into my mouth hitting the back of my throat. My eyes watering and tears streaming down my face.

He pulled my head back, wiped the tears from my face and pulled back.

"Be my dirty little whore."

He said, pushing me down on my knees and pulling me to him. Then spreading my legs, he started to finger my pussy. Hard and deep, two fingers and then soon his fist pounded me. It hurt, I squirmed almost pulling away. He yanked me back pounding me harder. My pussy now soaked and throbbing. I was ready to cum as I started to pant and moan with pleasure. Hearing this he stopped, denying me my orgasm.

"Not yet."

He said.

"You'll cum when I say so."

My pussy throbbing aching to cum as he moved to my ass. Then pushing his cock inch by inch he rammed it deep inside of me. My ass hurt, he was so deep and filled me so tight I was sure he could go no further and then he did. One hard thrust he went so deep a scream of pain shot from my throat. My pussy still aching to cum, as he started to violently rub my clit and encircle it with his thumb while still pounding my ass over and over.

My body completely lost in throws of passion as I started to moan and shriek with my arising orgasm. Once again he stopped, denying me once more.

"Beg me to cum."

He demanded and I complied.

"Oh please sir, please let me cum. I beg you sir, please, please let me cum."

I said.

Hearing my words quickly brought him to the heights of sexual satisfaction and his body raced ready to cum. He went hard at my clit, now wanting me to cum with him.

He grunted and groaned.

"Now you can cum. Cum my dirty little whore."

He yelled out as his body began to shake and he himself started to cum deep inside of my ass. Just as my orgasm began and my pussy pulsed so overly aroused I even squirted.

Now gasping to catch my breath, as he pulled out and my ass dripped.

I looked up to see the satisfied look on his face.

"Yes, yes"

He said.

"I think you're definitely the perfect woman for the job."

Helping me up from the floor, he kissed my cheek.

" I need the bathroom cleaned and my dinner ordered. Then you can take the night off."

He said and I agreed as he smacked my ass once more.

"Oh and."

"Yes sir."

I asked.

"Good job."

He said with a wink